The Wright Brothers

The Case of the Disappearing Acrobat
"It's Just Like the Circus!"

By MAURICE MILES MARTINEZ

1. African-Americans—Literature—United States 2. African-Americans—History—Modern ca. 1973-2009 3. Hip-hop—History—United States

iUniverse, Inc.
New York   Bloomington

The Wright Brothers
The Case of the Disappearing Acrobat
"It's Just Like the Circus!"

iUniverse books may be ordered through booksellers or by contacting:

iUniverse
1663 Liberty Drive
Bloomington, IN 47403
www.iuniverse.com
1-800-Authors (1-800-288-4677)

ISBN: 978-1-4502-4436-7 (pbk)
ISBN: 978-1-4502-4437-4 (ebk)

Library of Congress Control Number: 2010910205

Printed in the United States of America

iUniverse rev. date: 9/27/10

Cover Design by Maurice Miles Martinez

Acknowledgements

I would like to start by thanking the Most High and the Ancestors for taking me through the stages necessary to have the knowledge and understanding to write this book. It is the divine blessings of the Universe and the energy within that has brought me to inscribe this work. I would like to thank my mother for reading to me as a child and for contributing to the editing of this book. And I would like to thank my father for his creative spirit over the years that has inspired me and for editing this book.

About three years before this book was written, I heard a spoken word piece by the New York Poet named Phoenix. I credit this artist and poem for taking me down a direct path towards this book. His spoken word opened my mind to reengage much of the literature that my mother had shared with me and to conceive the idea for this work.

One of the main characters "Havier" was named after my son and I would like to thank him for his patience and creative spirit that contributed to the development of this character. Once this book was written, Beverly Dabrio offered the earliest editing and suggestions for which I am thankful. She made many suggestions that helped to develop this book and future Wright Brothers volumes. Another earlier reader who offered some of the most meaningful feedback was Roland Font. To him I am thankful for his African centered critique of this work and for the tactical suggestions about police and detective issues.

Amelia Yellin also gave this book a careful read and edited it, and Michael Yellin completed the painstakingly difficult task of editing it. I would like to thank both of the Yellins for their hard work, dedication and analysis of the book. This work would truly be different if it were not for their careful review.

I would like to thank my brother Torin Martinez for his review of the book and for his careful critique and suggestions to change some of the dialogue of the book. I would also like to thank Olayinka Fadahunsi for his cultural suggestions and Bonhomme for his careful analysis of the afterword and suggestions for the cover layout.

Special thanks goes out to Dr. William Seraile and to Dr. Bert Green. Both of these scholars were my professors. Dr. William Seraile took me through two master's degrees in Education and in History, and supervised the writing of my theses. One of my theses examined media views of Malcolm X over the decades and because it was written just prior to this book, I look upon it as the stone in the pyramid that elevated me to be able to write this book. I would also like to thank Dr. Seraile for his publication suggestions. Dr. Green too was a professor of mine who taught African Civilizations and served in an advisory role for some of the African cultural and historical portions of this work.

I would like to thank Michael Dabrio for his special assistance with the design of the cover. The cover would truly be different if it were not for his help. I would also like to thank Bevon Dabrio and Melissa Ruiz for their technical assistance with the acquisition of the cover image. I would like thank Jonathan Gaudette who offered the technical know-how to develop the cover of this book.

I would like to thank Rawle Charles, a novelist whose daily conversations with me about different directions to take with this work helped me to develop it further. He also played a unique role in reviewing, critiquing and editing the cover design and text when it was completed.

This work would be nothing without the lessons offered by the hip-hop artist KRS-One. His metaphysical lessons, taught through his music, lectures and live performances have helped to further develop my life and my writing. I encourage all to pursue these lessons with all due vigor because they will put you more in touch with yourself, the Universe, the Creator and the Ancestors. Peace and Blessings to all who read this book.

Contents

Chapter 1: Hip-Hop Ice on Ice 1

Chapter 2: The Wisdom of the Game... 6

Chapter 3: The Fire Drill... 14

Chapter 4: The Camera.. 19

Chapter 5: The Circus... 23

Chapter 6: The Precinct.. 33

Chapter 7: Questions and More Questions 41

Chapter 8: Guilty Acts 49

Chapter 9: The Magician's Riddle... 54

Chapter 10: A Physical Clue.. 62

Chapter 11: Back to the Circus 70

Chapter 12: A Conversation in the Park... 74

Chapter 13: Following the Animal Trainer 78

Chapter 14: A Test of the Equipment... 82

Chapter 15: A Magic Escape 92

Chapter 16: A Motive for the Crime 100

Chapter 17: A Revealing Conversation... 104

Chapter 18: An Attempted Mugging.. 109

Chapter 19: A DNA Match... 117

Chapter 20: Clearing Things Up 123

Chapter 21: Back to the Circus Store 128

Chapter 22: The Clarity of Comparison 132

Chapter 23: An Item of Interest 138

Chapter 24: An Unexpected Result 143

Chapter 25: True Fame... 156

Afterword.. 163

Chapter 1: Hip-Hop Ice on Ice

*****

The acrobat balanced delicately on what seemed to be the razor thin edge of the structure above. She had been through many acrobatic situations before, but this was by far the most dangerous. As she dangled from the edge of the cliff-like formation she wondered, "Why am I here? Will this be my end? Will I unwillingly fall from this enormous height to my final fate? For if it was my doing that placed me here, then fine."

She took one more glance toward the Earth below her and breathed in deeply. Sanctified, she tried to close her eyes and concentrate. For only through her own mind control could she attempt to take charge of the unstable physical situation and control her equilibrium. One wrong move would have made her kaleidoscope toward the Earth. One incorrect word or even the slightest sound might have made her life end there. As she tried to focus her mind, she momentarily lost concentration and fell as if pushed to the Earth. The fall was eternal but had a momentary briefness. As she was falling, someone from the crowd yelled, "Hit her!" Then all went dark and that was the last memory that she had.

*****

The Wright brothers sat in their Brooklyn living room discussing their father's cameras. He had so many: digital cameras, cameras with large flashes, cameras with long lenses that would allow you to zoom in close up from several miles away, and all sorts of video cameras. There must have been thirty in all.

Mr. Samuel Wright was a famous professional Black photographer. He had been responsible for capturing some of the greatest moments in African-American history. He often traveled to the African continent and to the Caribbean to photograph great African statesmen. Today Mr. Wright was visiting with a local advocate of union workers' rights by the name of Mr. L'Ouverture. Mr. L'Ouverture recently led a strike for better wages and was being jailed unjustly.

"I wonder how Dad is doing?" asked Havier.

At sixteen years of age Havier was two years older than his brother Marcus. Both Havier and Marcus were wise and well read young men. They knew all about the Civil Rights Movement that had helped to shape their parent's lives. They listened regularly to Malcolm X's speeches, but they also loved to listen to hip-hop music and were heavily into the culture. However, among the two, Havier thought about things more carefully than his brother Marcus.

"I bet he is asking Mr. L'Ouverture so many interesting questions," emphasized Havier.

"Yeah, and getting the best pictures!" responded Marcus.

"He probably has one of those pictures of Mr. L'Ouverture staring out in the distance like that famous picture of Dr. Martin Luther King that he took when he was young like us."

"Or maybe he'll take one of him and Mr. L'Ouverture with his camera on a timer."

Mr. Wright had several tripods on which he set up cameras to ensure that he would gain extra clear shots of a scene. Often, when on a photo shoot, he used the tripods and the timers to take pictures of himself and the person he was photographing. Mr. Wright also had a film studio set up in the basement of his home. The studio was complete with a darkroom for the development of pictures, special tools for editing film, two projectors, and two computers with the latest digital editing equipment.

"I can't wait to go to the circus," said Marcus while inserting one white headphone in his ear.

Marcus used white headphones to imitate those of the U'rGod. His father would not let him have a U'rGod. He said that they were too expensive, so Marcus and Havier both used inexpensive CD players.

"This Mos Bes is bumping," commented Marcus.

"Yeah underground hip-hop is where it's at! All these music videos they got on T.V. ain't nothing like the real stuff. The underground hip-hop artists that rock crowds on the reg are the best. Like the teacher of hip-hop, you know the one KRS, no one can rock like him," said Havier.

"Yeah, yeah I'm feeling that," said Marcus with a note of reluctance in his voice.

Despite their love for underground hip-hop, both Marcus and Havier were into clothing. They both wore the latest jeans and brand name boots. Nevertheless, at least Havier had a good understanding about where these things came from.

"It's a shame that they got all these sweat shops overseas in Latin America and Asia making these things."

"Yeah," added Marcus who knew much less about the subject than Havier.

"The way I see it is you got to wear something. I just don't see how they got us wearing these diamond earrings in both ears. Diamonds are a girl's best friend not mine. They got the Black man sissified and he don't even know it."

This made Marcus feel a little uncomfortable. He recently had his left ear pierced. Even though he had a generic stud in his ear, he was considering having the other ear pierced and buying cubic zirconiums for both ears. Marcus took off his novel era baseball cap, with the shinny new label and threw it on the couch next to him. Then he stood up with a twisted look on his face and began to adjust his durag.

"See those diamonds they got us wearing in our ears come from African blood mines. They are killing our brothers for the shine. It's so stupid. Fashion is fashion but murder is murder. And the music on T.V.," he went on, "all you see is people taking out chains and women shaking their behinds, that's not real hip-hop. That's a lie. A capitalist lie B."

"But all I want is the cubic zirconium. Nobody died for that," responded Marcus.

"Yo, let me break it down. Capitalism created slavery right? Capitalism created racism right? So any rap video that only promotes the get-the-money quick attitude is a manifestation of capitalism. It's modern day slavery and racism. You feeling me?"

"Yeah but…"

"But nothing, it's the get rich quick attitude. It's the fast money attitude, and when you got these big chains and earrings on, you are promoting it; cubic zirconium or not."

Marcus felt more uncomfortable and began to slouch in his chair. He lifted his hollow fake platinum necklace from its emblem and tucked it in his shirt.

"I wonder when Dad's going to get home," Marcus said.

"He said about 8:00 pm."

"I hope he brings us some of that gumbo from the African restaurant," replied Marcus.

"Yeah that's what I'm talking about," said Havier with a grin.

That night when their father got home he told them all about the day's activities over dinner. Yes, he had brought some African gumbo home. Their father told them about how Mr. L'Ouverture had a large number of supporters outside of his jail cell. Mr. Wright explained that he had the chance to take several pictures of the men who stood outside the prison where the union official was being kept.

"I met Mr. Al Sharpman," he told his sons. Mr. Sharpman was a famous advocate for Black peoples' rights. He had grown from a local activist to become a nationally recognized leader, and even ran for president of the United States. Mr. Sharpman was known all over the United States as one of the most articulate speakers. Although Mr. Wright had interacted with many Black leaders, this was his first time speaking with Mr. Sharpman. "He set up a candlelight vigil for Mr. L'Ouverture. I know this will help to attract media attention. Some of my pictures might end up in the New York papers. So how was your day boys?" asked Mr. Wright.

"Ok," responded Havier.

Marcus was silent.

"How about you Marcus? How was your day?"

"Fine," replied Marcus.

"Just fine and ok," stated their father. "Those words are so non-descriptive. It's like saying that the dinner we are eating is plain. What if I came home after such an exciting day and told you that my day was fine or ok? You guys would be mad at me if I said that I didn't do much today."

"Yeah, but we didn't do much," said Marcus.

"Never minimize what you do. Every motion that you take on this planet we call Earth has a purpose and is very important. So what motions did you take today?" asked their father with a gentle tone.

"I don't know," Marcus said while shrugging his shoulders.

"Did you do your homework boys?"

Havier enthusiastically explained, "I did mine Dad. We're working on this science project that deals with the concept of Newton's law of gravity.

Did you know that all objects fall to the Earth at the same rate? That is if you account for no wind resistance. For example, if you drop a bowling ball and a marble from a cliff they will hit the ground at exactly the same time. Anyway, I had some formulas to complete for physics homework and an essay to write for English. I started them on the bus and completed them as soon as we got home while Marcus was watching T.V."

The last part of what Havier said slipped out of his mouth.

"And how about you Marcus?" inquired their father.

"I didn't have much homework today," he said in a guilty tone.

"Much? What does that mean? What subjects gave you homework?"

"Math and social studies."

"Did you do it?"

"Well I started my math during the last period because we had a substitute for gym class and we just sat there but…"

He was interrupted by the doorbell ringing.

"But what?" their father stayed with the thought.

"I didn't get to do it yet."

"Please complete your homework now," stated Mr. Wright firmly.

Havier headed toward the door to open it. "One minute," he said to the person on the outside. "Who's there?" Havier asked.

"It's Mr. Lawson."

Havier opened the door because he recognized the voice. Mr. Lawson was their neighbor.

"Hey Samuel!" said Mr. Lawson to Mr. Wright. "I got that book you were looking for," he said handing him a copy of a book titled: 'Historic Black Photography.'

"Thanks," smiled Mr. Wright.

"Well, I got to go."

"See you later."

By now Marcus had started his homework. He was writing an essay comparing Langston Hughes' cultural consciousness to that of Malcolm X.

Marcus worked hard for the next two hours. By eleven he had completed his work and both of the Wright brothers went to bed.

Chapter 2: The Wisdom of the Game

The following day nothing out of the ordinary happened at school. The Wright brothers went to class and Marcus was happy that he had his homework completed. During gym class Marcus played football. Havier didn't have gym class that day because he was in the eleventh grade. Marcus, who was in ninth grade, had gym class on Tuesdays and Thursdays. Havier had gym class on Mondays and Wednesdays.

The Wright brothers had about a twenty-five minute bus ride home every day. At the end of the day both of the young men boarded the bus. Marcus went to sleep. An argument between two students woke Marcus up for a few minutes, but it soon ended and he drifted off to sleep again.

This Tuesday was a nice spring day in April. The hum of the bus as it passed by grassy parks in Brooklyn was somewhat soothing in an artificial way. Marcus often dozed off on the ride home. Today he seemed extra tired, and slept on the bus while Havier started his homework. After a few minutes, Havier reached a problem in his physics homework that was giving him a good deal of trouble.

"I wonder how I'm going to complete this problem," thought Havier to himself. "I guess I will have to run this by a classmate or…"

The bus hit a bump. It was one of those rather large speed bumps placed to slow down cars to about fifteen miles per hour. These bumps were about four or five times the size of regular speed bumps. They were often placed on roads that ran near school zones. Their purpose was to slow down traffic during school hours, not to bring it to a five mile per hour crawl like regular speed bumps. There were many of these speed bumps throughout the city's streets and they occupied so much of the street that drivers even had to slow down for them at other times of the day.

As the bus hit the bump it felt as though it was suspended in the air for a second. And then it hit the ground with and abrupt "bang!"

"He must have been doing forty or forty-five miles per hour when he hit that one," Havier thought. He hesitated for a second and exclaimed inwardly, "That's the answer to my physics problem!"

Havier had been trying to compute a complicated problem concerning the motion of different objects. The bus hitting the bump helped him to conceptualize the problem. Both brothers loved to figure out problems in nature and this physics problem was certainly one of them. They liked to ask questions such as why shadows looked longer when the sun was at a different place in the sky or why most people in Christopher Columbus' era should have known like the ancient Africans that the Earth was round just by looking at the bend in the horizon and by studying astronomy.

"Marcus, wake up. This is our stop," Havier said as he put his physics notebook in his book bag.

Marcus got up from his slumber and drearily strolled off the bus behind Havier.

After a five minute walk home Marcus was a little more alive. As they walked up the steps of their brownstone they heard the loud clang-bang of a jackhammer. Apparently some construction was taking place on their block. The power company was using the jackhammer to break through the concrete.

"Open the door," Marcus said with an anxious tone. "I want to get something to eat."

Marcus went straight to the refrigerator while Havier went to the shelf and grabbed a book.

"Dad's coming home early Marcus. Make sure you get your homework done. You remember what happened last night."

"Yeah, I know you sold me out yesterday," Marcus said while reaching into his book bag.

"I didn't mean to sell you out. What I said just slipped out."

Marcus took out a math book and notebook and began to work on some algebra problems.

Havier joined him. After completing their homework, they grabbed their basketball and went to the park to shoot some hoops.

Their good friends Eugene and Damien were at the park. Eugene's father was a doctor. Damien's mother taught for the Department of Education. She was a high school social studies teacher. Damien was always into the latest fashions.

"I got the new Gordens," he told the Wright brothers, "Check them out." The young men stared as if in awe. The sneakers were white with a shiny blue section.

"You know what's deep about all these shoes? They got us buying plastic and leather for one hundred fifty…" emphasized Havier as he was cut off by Damien.

"I paid one forty-five for mine," Damien said proudly with a smile.

"That's not what I mean," Havier said with an annoyed tone. "They got us buying these Gordens, jackets, expensive jeans, fake diamond earrings for all kind of money that we don't have."

"What you mean?" asked Eugene. "You got seventy-five dollar jeans on and Toms on your feet."

"That's true, but…"

"But nothing," replied Damien, "Toms is Toms and Gordens is Gordens. You're just jealous because you don't have the Gordens." He grabbed the basketball which had been resting on the ground and took a perfect shot that was nothing but net.

"Well what I'm trying to say is that when we over focus on shoes that are made in sweat shops, we are worshiping them and that's negative. This is just some of the stuff we should pay attention to," started Havier.

"Some of the stuff, or all of the stuff, or just the stuff you don't like, or do like? Which one is it Havier? You can't have it both…"

Just then Mr. Billings approached. Mr. Billings was one of the elders in the community. He must have been somewhere in his late fifties or early sixties, yet he appeared not a day over forty-eight. He had such a presence. He held himself as a commanding African-American man, but he also had a gentle side and when Mr. Billings spoke he just made so much sense. It was as though he had some kind of magical power. He really made you understand the true meaning of life and he understood the youth better than anyone.

Havier really admired Mr. Billings. Sometimes, when Mr. Billings would visit the family he would have conversations with him about what books he should be reading next. Mr. Billings had read all kinds of interesting books during his lifetime. He was like a walking library.

"I heard you young men talking about Gordens," said Mr. Billings with a smile. "See style in the Black community, comes from where?"

The boys listened, intently hanging on every word.

Mr. Billings continued, "You see that tree? It needs nothing more than what it is born with. But you see that white mark on it. Do you know what it means?"

The boys responded in unison, "No."

"A man put it there. They're going to cut down that tree because they feel it's not healthy. Don't let that mark be placed on you young men."

"Now do you see that woman?" Mr. Billings pointed across the street to a woman who was pouring some black potting soil into a flower pot containing a budding rose she just planted. "She's nurturing that plant with nature's finest. And although she's covering the base of it in the same way that the tree base is covered with paint, she is giving it life."

The young men had grown fascinated by Mr. Billings' explanation.

"Fashion can be like that mark on the tree forecasting your downfall, or like that soil enriching your experiences in life."

"Didn't you wear fashions in your day Mr. Billings?" asked Damien with an inquiring tone.

"Yes we did young man. But in my day we wore fashions that, for the most part, helped to connect us with our roots. We wore our hair in afros, we wore dashikis and we talked about empowerment for the community. Today we talk about gaining wealth for ourselves. The fashion is geared toward unattainable wealth. We never had that in the community. No diamond earrings, no big platinum chains, no fifty pairs of one hundred-fifty dollar sneakers."

This time Damien did not protest about the cost of the Gorden's he was wearing. It was something about how Mr. Billings put things.

"See these material objects are an attempt to get you to go to jail because everyone can't be a professional basketball player and everyone can't be a rap star making millions. So what do we have left? To become a hustler, and that means illegal activity. You see how we are set up to fail?" Mr. Billings continued, "Did you know that fifty percent of Black men on any given basketball court think they can play ball in the professional league? But only one in ten thousand will actually play. That's a trap. I'll see you fellows later."

Mr. Billings strolled over and picked up the basketball from where it was resting beyond the three point line and took a shot. "Swish!" the ball went through the hoop as the net flew up.

"Still got it with no Gorden's 'cause I can't afford them."

The teens laughed. Mr. Billings had a wonderful sense of humor. He would always leave you with a warm feeling about yourself.

"You young men stay away from trouble now. You're all very nice young men and I don't want to see you getting hurt. Especially out here when someone puts a move on you like…" Mr. Billings dribbled the ball switching it back and forth between hands as he ran to the hoop, did a spin and made a successful lay-up. "See ya'll later."

"Bye Mr. Billings," the young men responded in unison.

They started their game of basketball. The two Wright brothers played two on two against Eugene and Damien.

Damien was slightly taller than Havier. He was the only one of the four who could slam dunk. Because of this, and his fascination with his Gorden's, he liked to dunk and to hog the ball. This often made his teammates jealous and is one of the reasons that Havier and Marcus preferred not to be on his team.

"Don't hog the ball Damien," said Eugene at the start of the game.

"Don't worry, I won't."

Surprisingly, Damien did not keep the ball to himself. In fact, he passed it to Eugene more than Havier and Marcus passed it to one another. Perhaps, Mr. Billings had an impact on Damien's selfishness. Whatever was the case, Damien was much more sharing than he usually was. In fact, he didn't even try to dunk once in the game.

The game was to twenty-one. Each shot was worth two points unless it was a three point basket. Damien dribbled did a spin move and then passed the ball out to Eugene who was wide open. Both Havier and Marcus had double teamed Damien.

"All net!" Eugene exclaimed as he gave Damien a traditional African handshake.

The game went back and forth. Amazingly, Havier stuffed Damien. At this, all three young men chanted an, "Oh!"

It was twenty to eighteen. Damien and Eugene were ahead. Marcus stole the ball from Eugene. He passed it to Havier, and then Havier passed it back. Marcus drove to the hoop with Eugene covering him. He flipped it back to Havier and Havier shot. The ball hit the backboard, bounced off the rim and Marcus grabbed the rebound. He was open, jumped up in the air and shot the ball.

"Whoosh!" the ball ripped through the net.

Now it was tied. The game had to be won by two shots and Havier and Marcus had the ball. Havier started after the check and put a move on Eugene who was covering him. He passed the ball to Marcus, and Marcus passed it back to Havier. Havier drove to the hoop, tripped, and Damien swatted the ball out of his hand. It flew quickly away from Havier, but Damien had hit it so hard that it kept going. Both Damien and Eugene eyed the ball. It hit the ground and was bouncing rapidly towards Marcus. Both of them started toward Marcus.

By now Havier had begun to get up. Marcus saw this out of the corner of his eye. He flipped the ball high in the air to Havier and he took the lay-up. The ball bounced off the backboard and went straight through the net.

"It's twenty-two to twenty! Point game!" said Havier.

"Bring it then!" said Eugene.

Havier dribbled up to the net. Both Damien and Eugene guarded their opponents very carefully. Havier drove to the hoop and he was double-teamed by Damien and Eugene. He took a jump shot. Damien jumped high in the air and rejected the shot. Eugene grabbed the ball and drove to the hoop. Marcus came over and tried to slow him down. Eugene jumped and put a spin move on Marcus. Marcus went up as high as he could in the air. He felt the tip of his middle finger catch Eugene's shot.

The ball seemed suspended in air for an eternity. As it drifted in slow motion toward the hoop, it hit the rim, began to spin around it in a counter clockwise motion and then it flew out.

Marcus grabbed the rebound and passed the ball out to Havier. The Wright brothers worked in an organized unison. Every motion had a purpose. Havier passed the ball behind his back to Marcus. Havier slowly backed up to the hoop while he was guarded by Damien. Marcus was further back, carefully guarded closely by Eugene. Suddenly, Havier made a spin move toward the hoop. Elevated, he passed the ball to Marcus, who was standing beyond the three point line.

For some strange reason, both Damien and Eugene bolted toward Marcus. Marcus looked as though he was not concerned with the game as if he was standing at the foul line gearing up for a shot. He aimed, but Damien and Eugene were upon him. Marcus jumped and tried to launch the ball over Damien and Eugene. This was almost an impossible feat especially when one takes into account the fact that Damien could jump the highest on the court.

The ball sailed over both opponents' hands, missing the top of Damien's hand by two inches. Havier watched it as it glided in an ark toward the rim. It flew down and, "Swish!"

"Right on little brother!" commented Havier.

"Twenty-five to twenty!" said Marcus.

"Marcus we got to get home, it's 6:15. Dad's going to be home soon." The young men had been at the court for about an hour.

"Peace," Havier gave Damien and Eugene an African handshake.

"Peace," Marcus said to Damien and Eugene with a similar embrace.

The Wright brothers headed toward their home. They talked about the game on the way. When they got home, their father hadn't arrived yet, but their mother was home from work and was cooking dinner. Their mother, Olivia Wright was an independent contractor. She helped advise organizations on how to become more efficient. She worked for some of the largest humanitarian organizations. Occassionally, she also worked for private companies.

"Hi, Mom," said Havier.

"Hello, your father will be home in about fifteen minutes. How was your day?" said Mrs. Wright.

"Pretty good Mom," Havier replied.

"My day went well too. I'm currently working for this client that is making an effort to get reverends and ministers to make hip-hop an important part of their churches."

"Wow, that's heavy Mom," Marcus replied.

"Yes, I thought it was a wonderful cause and it's a great way to reach the youth," their mother observed.

"Maybe the only way to reach the youth," Havier added.

The young men washed up for dinner and looked forward to their father's return. Mr. Wright came in the door.

"Hi Dad!" the Wright brothers exclaimed.

"How are my two sons doing?"

"Great!"

"That's what I like to hear! Did you boys do your homework yet?"

"Yes!" responded Marcus with enthusiasm.

"I'm glad to hear that," said their father.

The family sat down to eat dinner and the conversation continued.

"Did you photograph anyone famous today Dad?" asked Havier.

"Yeah, I went back to the protest outside of Mr. L'Ouverture's jail cell. Several hip-hop activists and artists had joined the vigil. They said that they wanted to show solidarity with their fellow black union activist," said their father.

"There were artists there?" asked Marcus.

"Yes, all types of politically conscious artists."

"I know your father went back because the protest has been growing," added Mrs. Wright.

"That's right! All the radical hip-hop leaders and activists were at the protest. You know, not these clowns that they have on these music videos; showing off their chains and earrings and all of that foolishness. But people who are really about something in life other than a capitalist search for self-wealth," Mr. Wright said in a firm tone.

"Yes, I agree Samuel but that's the language we must speak in order to reach the youth today," said Mrs. Wright.

"Well, I'm fine with speaking the language of hip-hop if it means upliftment," Mr. Wright responded.

"When it started during the first two decades of the 1970's through the early 1990's that's what it meant Samuel. It meant victory over the streets. It didn't mean to become some thug with one hundred thousand dollars of jewelry on your wrist. You remember those times Samuel."

"Yes I do and how things have changed."

The family continued to eat dinner and to discuss hip-hop and its historical role as a protest movement. After dinner the Wright brothers got their clothes ready for the next day. Havier read a chapter in his favorite book: *The Autobiography of Malcolm X* and Marcus watched music videos.

After awhile Marcus went into the room where Havier was reading, sat down on an adjacent bed and asked him, "What you doing?"

It was obvious that Havier was reading. However, Marcus was bored and needed a conversation starter.

"What's the matter, you got bored watching those music videos?" Havier asked.

"Yeah, kind of," Marcus said with some hesitation in his voice.

"Check this book out, I just finished it last week. It's called: *From Superman to Man*. It's about this Black porter back in the days of Jim Crow segregation who schools this racist White American senator. It's one of the best books I've read yet," said Havier while tossing Marcus the book.

Marcus opened it, began reading and yawned. Within a few minutes, he had fallen asleep.

Havier continued reading for another half an hour before resting his book on the nightstand next to the bed, turning off the lamp and going to sleep.

Chapter 3: The Fire Drill

The day was Wednesday. The middle of the week was always a happy time for the Wright brothers. It meant that the week was half over and that the weekend was approaching. The brothers woke up earlier that day than they usually did.

"I can't wait for today's school spring fair," Marcus exclaimed.

The school fair always took place during this time of year. Havier asked his father if he could borrow one of his older model digital cameras. His father agreed.

It was actually a fair that took place on the basketball courts of the school gym. As soon as Havier entered the fairground he began to take pictures of everything and he continued to do so throughout the day. During the spring fair the staff at the school set up tables and booths in the gym and invited all types of vendors who sold various kinds of trinkets.

There were a variety of game booths in which you could win prizes. For example, there was a booth where you would try to knock down three pins with baseballs. You got four baseballs in all. If you won, you'd receive one of those stuffed animals that looked like an oversized rabbit, but wasn't really that type of animal.

There was also one of those booths containing hundreds of bottles. You would receive ten rings and would have to get one of them to land on the bottle top. It seemed like an easy enough task, so Marcus tried it.

"Hav watch this, ten out of ten prizes," Marcus boasted as he threw the ring toward the bottles.

The ring bounced and Havier laughed. "Maybe on the next try Marcus."

Marcus tossed another ring while saying, "Nine out of nine." The ring bounced off of the bottles again.

Havier teased Marcus again, "Try none out of ten, or maybe one if you're lucky."

"It's not luck, it's skill. Trust me Hav."

Marcus threw a few more rings. Finally, he got one on when he only had two rings left in his hand. This was exceptional because all of the other students were tossing rings and not getting a single one on the bottles.

"See I told you Havier, it's all in the touch of the toss!" Marcus said bragging.

"We have a winner!" the woman inside the booth yelled. "Here is your prize. If you get another one on you can trade in that prize for one of the big stuffed animals."

"Here it goes. One out of two, one out of two," Marcus tossed the ring; it bounced off of one bottle top, landed on another, and then bounced off of that one too. "Man!" he exclaimed in disappointment, but then he quickly rebounded. "I got one out of one. Here it comes!" He said as he threw the ring which landed upright, flew way up in the air and then landed right on top of one of the bottles.

"We have another winner! Trade that stuffed animal in and I'll give you a big one," the woman announced.

"See I told you I could do it, Hav. It only takes a little drive!" said Marcus.

There was also one of those dunk the clown booths at the school fair. The booth contained a clown who wore a red hat, a big red nose and had a face that was covered in some thick white paste. The clown wore a purple hat, had large green shoes with twisted laces and he wore a purple and orange polka dot jacket. Near the front of the line a short, stocky white man stood collecting the money from students who were trying to dunk the clown.

"The best thing about all of the games is that they only cost a quarter," said Havier.

"Yeah, yeah," Marcus agreed.

The high school had hired the fair. Therefore, most of the expenses had been covered by the principal.

All of a sudden, "Boom!" Someone dunked the clown. When this happened the contraption he was sitting on made a noise and he was released into a pool of water below.

"That was hot!" said Marcus.

"I think I might try that a little later," said Havier.

He had already been dunked several times for the day. In fact, it was evident that the paint on his face had undergone some wear and tear. This time when he was dunked, the thick layer of paste flew off of his face. The man underneath looked remarkably different than the clown mask. He had blonde hair and blue eyes. His hair was straight, stringy and he had a light brown moustache. He had a weird look on his face after losing his makeup.

The clown grudgingly got back on the dunk platform without his makeup on. The mask was made up of some sort of thick plaster-like material that had been painstakingly applied in layers to the clown's face. Therefore, it could not easily be put back on. This would involve an elaborate makeup/mask job that would take hours.

"It's strange," said Havier with a grin.

"What's strange?" replied Marcus.

"I mean that man in the clown suit. Seeing that man there in the clown suit, I was just thinking."

"Thinking what?" asked Marcus with an anxious tone.

"I was thinking that they used to have us in those clown suits. You know the minstrel shows where they would have a Black man on the stage in blackface who was made to look ignorant."

"Yeah, so that's a white clown."

"Well there have always been white clowns, but a clown shouldn't make fun of someone because of his/her race."

"I'm feeling that Hav," Marcus said in a lackluster way trying to avoid the conversation.

"Yeah that's what I'm saying. Back in the day, they would have some degrading image of us kissing up to some slave master in the movies. Then I was thinking that they still do have us in these minstrel shows. Just look at the state of hip-hop today. All these brothers talking about how much bread they got and that's the whole content of their rhymes. And then the big diamond earrings. You know I was up in the Bronx the other day on Fordham Road doing some shopping and one of the jewelry stores there has a coon on the front."

"A what?"

"A coon, you know one of these stereotypical images of a Black man with big bulging eyes. And do you know what he had on the end of his hand?"

"No, what?"

"He had a big diamond ring. And he was grinning with that coon grin."

"For real?" asked Marcus

"Word is bond!" replied Havier. "You see we can't even identify racist images when they're right in front of us. We're buying jewelry from a store that's making fun of us."

"I'm feeling that," responded Marcus.

All of a sudden, the Wright brother's conversation was interrupted by a bell.

"Ding!" "Ding!" "Ding!" "Ding!"

Then a silent pause.

"Ding!" "Ding!" "Ding!" "Ding!"

There was a fire drill! The students slowly filed outside. Hundreds of students stood outside of the building. Marcus wondered if they would be allowed to go back inside so that they could have fun at the fair. Most fire drills took five or ten minutes time before the school staff would allow the students back inside.

The minutes ticked by and Havier and Marcus waited. The bell to change classes rang inside and outside of the building. By now, the students began to wonder why they hadn't been allowed back into the building. After a few more minutes, firemen arrived and a teacher announced that there had been a fire at the rear of the building. Apparently, a furnace in the basement had caught on fire. The smoke had been trapped in the basement. However, now it was apparent because smoke was seeping out through some of the basement windows, and from some of the classroom windows.

The firemen entered the building to extinguish the flames. Apparently the fire was relatively localized at one furnace because they were able to put it out within a few minutes. However, because the fire had burned for so long, most of the school building was filled with smoke. Therefore, the remainder of the activities that day were canceled and the children were sent home.

This posed only a minor problem for both the students and school officials. By the time the announcement was made, it was seventh period and the day was almost over. The fire had actually occurred toward the end of fifth period and the children had waited more than one period for the announcement. Since most New York City students take public transportation to school, the pupils were able to get home on their own by taking the busses and subways. A few students took specialized services busses home, but the busses had already arrived to wait until the normal day was done. These busses were able to take the teens home on their regular schedule.

The Wright brothers got on the bus that took them home. Today there was someone talking extra loud on their cellular phone.

"I'm sorry that fire drill happened," said Marcus.

"Me too," Havier responded.

"That fair was hot!"

"Yeah, why did a fire have to happen on the one day that the fair came to school?"

"I feel you."

The brothers went home relaxed, read and did their homework.

Chapter 4: The Camera

The fire in the school made the week a little more unusual than the Wrights expected. What made the week even more special was the Black circus which took place that weekend. To the Wright brothers the Black circus was a special event!

"A circus like no other!" said Marcus

"Too bad it only comes to town once a year," said Havier.

"Yeah but then again most circuses only come to town about once a year."

"I've been looking forward to going to the circus for at least three months."

"Me too!" responded Marcus.

As their anticipation built they thought of all of the exciting things that the circus had in store for them. There were acrobats from Ethiopia, and many clowns. There was a magician that did all kinds of wonderful tricks. There were trained lions and tigers that did tricks, dancing horses and several very large elephants. There was a little dog that rode around on a larger grey dog. The rhythmic drum beats produced by the circus musicians made the Black circus come alive.

The lively spirit of the circus was similar to Black marching bands or the Djembe drum players of West Africa. That's where these drum beats came from. Of course Havier had a better understanding of this concept than did Marcus. But nevertheless, both young men enjoyed the Black circus.

"Can I please use your brand new Supermaxtronic 3000 digital camera Dad?" Havier asked in a pleading tone.

"We'll be very careful with it," Marcus added.

"I promise we'll be extra careful like we were with your other camera last year."

The camera that they wanted to borrow was their father's newest digital camera. It cost thousands of dollars. Normally, this would not have been a problem, but two years prior the Wright brothers had borrowed one of their father's cameras and virtually destroyed it.

While riding the train to the circus, the two young men started playing a dangerous game. They were riding in between the subway train cars. As the cars jolted back and forth, Marcus, who was holding the camera, dropped it and began to fall to his knees to grab it.

The camera had a strap with one of those snap-on hooks. Marcus had it fastened to one of the loops on his jeans. As Marcus fell to his knees, the camera got trapped between the subway cars. The strap got entangled in some moving part of the train and Marcus was being pulled toward the moving gap between the two cars.

"Havier help!" Marcus screamed.

The gap between the two cars looked like a shark's mouth ready to swallow him alive.

Havier grabbed Marcus underneath the arms, looped his hands around Marcus' shoulders and screamed, "I'm trying!"

A tug-of war ensued between Havier and the shark-mouthed train.

"Pull!" yelled Marcus.

"I am!" his brother responded.

To Havier it seemed as though an eternity was passing and he had lost the battle.

"It's pulling me in!" Marcus yelled.

Marcus was only inches from becoming train food. Havier braced himself and with one big heave, he lurched back. However, the pull of the train was too much. Marcus' pants loop was now entering the gobbling train mouth.

"It's about to pinch my side! That'll be it for me!"

Then all of a sudden, "Snap!" All of that pulling had broken Marcus' belt loop. The Wright brothers stood up and went back inside the train. Later they told their father what happened. He was very concerned for the safety of his sons. That was the first year that he had allowed them to go to the circus by themselves.

Mr. Wright filed a report with the authorities so that they would look for his camera. It was found a few weeks later by a track worker.

Although, the mangled camera was barely recognizable, Mr. Wright was very thankful to God that his son had not been injured.

It was this incident that made Mr. Wright somewhat apprehensive about lending his newest camera to his sons. The year after the big incident, the Wright brothers got to borrow a camera, but it was one of Mr. Wright's older less expensive models. This year they wanted to borrow his best camera.

"Please can we borrow the Supermaxtronic 3000? We were good with your camera last year," said Marcus.

"I hope you boys learned your lesson two years ago. You could have been killed!"

"Yes, Dad," said Havier in a remorseful tone, "We're still very sorry about what we did."

"We were young then," Marcus continued, "And we didn't know any better."

"I think you did know better, and one day you will look back on this conversation and see that you are still very young." Mr. Wright said in a stern tone. Then he smiled but spoke in a firm tone. He hoped that his son's would someday incorporate photography and reporting into their careers and this was a perfect opportunity to encourage them. "I am going to let you two take the Supermaxtronic 3000 camera if you promise to take good care of it, and if you break it, you agree to replace it."

"We promise. Thanks Dad!" the Wright brothers said in unison.

"Now don't you go out there trying to be some sort of super heroes taking photographs of anything and everything," Mr. Wright said laughing as he often did with his signature sense of humor.

"We won't Dad," Marcus replied.

This time Mr. Wright spoke a little more seriously, "There are a few new features on this camera that you should know about. The digital imagery is so refined that even small sections of wide angled images that are taken from several miles away can be brought into focus. The camera can see objects one-sixteenth of an inch in length from several miles away. There is also a video feature to the camera, but I'm still learning it myself and you don't have to worry about it."

Mr. Wright and his sons went downstairs to the studio. He plugged the camera into one of the computers in his studio. He loaded several images that he had snapped from the Brooklyn Bridge. They were of Manhattan's skyline with the sun setting behind it. Using the computer, Mr. Wright zoomed in further on one particular rooftop. As the zoom got closer, the other buildings became blurry and disappeared off of the sides of the screen.

"Hot!" exclaimed Marcus.

Mr. Wright continued to zoom in until his sons could see that there was a small crane-like machine on the roof and little men standing next to it. The professional photographer selected one of the men and zoomed in on him. He was a construction worker like the other men and had on an orange hard hat. Zooming in on him, it looked as though he was putting a silver circular object into a blue and white checkered bag. His other arm was blocking part of the object. Mr. Wright zoomed in on the worker's face.

Marcus commented, "That guy looks familiar."

"Like a construction worker," Havier teased Marcus with a chuckle.

"No, I've seen him before."

By now Mr. Wright had zoomed in on the worker's eyes. One of his eyelids was closed, the other half open. The image was so refined that you could see each and every one of the worker's eyelashes.

"Wow! That's a hot camera Dad!" said Marcus. "It will be great for the circus. We'll take extra good care of it!"

The young men went to sleep that night with anticipation for the circus. They woke up extra early even though it was a Saturday morning. They went and got breakfast. Carefully, they took their father's camera and put it in the padded carrying case.

Their father had left a note on the bag which read: "Take Heed, be careful or you will pay for it!"

The camera also had a large storage unit which held the digital imagery. The unit contained ten high capacity hard drives and rested comfortably in the carrying bag. Havier placed the strap across his chest and rested the bag on his hip.

On the walk to the subway Marcus said, "Hey Havier, you want to take the camera out to try it?"

"No!" responded Havier with an angry temperament. "You know what Dad said. We have to take good care of his camera."

Havier placed an arm on his father's camera bag.

"Could you be any more careful with that bag?" Marcus asked sarcastically. "It's not like you're guarding Fort Knox or something."

"We'll, it is Dad's newest camera and we said we would take good care of it," responded Havier.

"Yeah, I guess you're right," said Marcus.

The Wright brothers walked down the stairs into the subway.

Chapter 5: The Circus

The Black circus took place in the Bronx and was more than an hour's ride from Brooklyn. It would be in town for the next five weeks with a total of six weekend shows, including this one. The circus had an early show and an evening show on both Saturdays and Sundays. Five weeks was an unusually long time for a circus to visit one city. However, the Black circus was suffering financially and it always drew large crowds when it came to New York City. Therefore, its management decided that an extended stay in the city was warranted. Except for a few people selling small trinkets to the train riders, individuals preaching their version of the word of God, and a few unfortunate people who were asking for money, the train trip was not out of the ordinary. Of course, there was also the man who sold M&M's on the train.

The M&M man always entered the subway car holding a massive box in his arms. He placed it on the floor, reached in with both hands and pulled out two bunches of three packs. He proceeded to walk up and down the subway car in a staccato manner announcing, "Not one M&M, not two M&M's, but three juicy delicious M&M's for one dollar!"

Surprisingly between five and ten people would signal the man and make a purchase. When the train stopped at a station, the M&M man would exit the train and enter another train car. Havier did the math one day and found out that if the man made a fifty-percent profit on each sale, that he would have made between $2.50 and $5.00 per car. That equaled an average of seventy-five cents per minute or about $43.00 per hour.

"Not a bad living," Havier told his younger brother.

"Yeah, $43.00 an hour is not bad!" Marcus added.

"The only problem is getting arrested for selling stuff illegally on the train," affirmed Havier.

"That's illegal? You mean he stole those M&M's?"

"Of course he didn't steal them. But you're not supposed to sell things on the train. Didn't he look a little nervous to you?"

"Yeah, he must have a rap sheet a mile long. Who wants that kind of a life? Dad's is much better!" exclaimed Marcus.

Nothing really happened during the remainder of the ride. It was the normal hustle bustle of the city. People pushed to get on and off the train. People were squeezing together and more unfortunate souls trying to evade the trap that society had placed them in asked for money.

"You know what's funny?" said Havier.

"What?" Marcus replied in an inquisitive tone.

"This city is really defined by both racial diversity and racism. All you have to do is look at this train ride. Once you get above eighty-sixth street in Manhattan the white folks become less and less," Havier thought out loud.

"Until you don't see none!"

"Or maybe just one. Unless there's a baseball game then you see a whole bunch of white people."

"You fellows are really on point," added an elder African-American gentleman who was standing nearby. The man had a graying beard and was wearing a red, black and green beaded necklace. "And many other times you see people like that," he motioned toward a white passenger dressed in a suit, "coming to the Bronx or Harlem to pick up the money from the business he owns there. If that doesn't seem strange to you, just imagine yourself trying to open up a soul food restaurant in their neighborhood."

"That's right. The man would run you out of there!" exclaimed Havier.

"Too bad it has to be that way," Marcus added in a depressed tone of voice as the Wright brothers' stop was quickly approaching.

"See you latter Mr.," said Havier.

"Take care young men."

After exiting the train Marcus said, "I can't wait to see this circus!"

Havier agreed, "Yeah I know it'll be hot!"

They got there early and so they had to wait until the circus gates opened. The Wright brothers entered the arena where the circus was being held. They had good seats in the middle of the arena and about half way down to the floor. Their early arrival meant another wait before the circus started.

The circus began with a bang! The drum beats kept it so alive. The ringmaster came out and began to announce as the magnificent show began. There were Ethiopian, West African and African-American acrobats flipping high in the air. The acrobats flew from one trapeze to another while doing summersaults in the air.

There were horses and elephants with large, splendid bridles that were fastened to their backs and undersides. Throughout the show they circled the arena and were led by clowns. Often there was one clown riding in addition to the one leading the elephant.

Clowns danced around the arena. Acrobats seemed to fly through the air. There were four massive trampolines in the arena. They were placed under the trapezes. One of the clowns had an outfit with a drum on the back of it. She was on the floor helping the ringmaster.

A magician was also in the arena. He motioned toward one of the trapezes with his arms. A huge bang was followed by a puff of smoke which appeared around an acrobat who was flying midair between the trampoline and the trapeze. Within a few seconds the smoke was gone and the acrobat had disappeared in thin air! About one minute later, several other bangs and puffs of smoke appeared. Then a group of clowns came forward and danced as the crowd became excited and cheered.

When the clowns stepped away from the center of the stage, the magician made a few more gestures and swung his arms toward another trampoline on the other side of the arena. Another large bang filled the arena followed by another puff of smoke which appeared slightly above the trampoline. The acrobat that had just disappeared flew up from the puff of smoke in a flip and grabbed the trapeze above. The crowd screamed with enthusiasm.

The magician waved his arms again and another acrobat disappeared with a puff of smoke. Then two more bangs came with a gesture of his arms and yet another acrobat, and then another disappeared behind clouds of smoke. The drums and music filled the arena and only increased the crowd's anticipation and excitement. The magician waved his arms again and again. More loud bangs and puffs of smoke were created by the magician and the acrobats appeared one-by-one behind them. The crowd cheered and the magician took a bow.

The magician made the acrobats disappear and reappear several times from thin air. Then he waved his arms and the acrobats disappeared for good one by one.

During the entire first half of the circus Marcus was taking pictures with his father's camera. He began to snap feverishly as the circus progressed.

"Let me get the camera!" Havier said in an anxious voice.

"During the second half of the show you can get it!" Marcus exclaimed while he kept snapping pictures.

"The second half?" replied Havier, "You better give me the camera!"

"I said after the intermission!" Marcus argued angrily.

"Look, look you're messing up the pictures by shaking the camera!"

"That's because you keep bothering me about getting your turn."

To some extent, both of the Wright brothers were telling the truth. They argued for some time about who would get the camera and when. Surprisingly, Marcus got to keep the camera for the remainder of the first half.

Eventually Havier conceded, "Well, after the intermission it's mine and I hope you don't try to get it during the second half of the show. Remember that, you just remember that."

"Whatever," Marcus said while he captured the show on the digital imagery of the Supermaxtronic 3000 camera.

During their conversation, the magician was making the acrobats disappear. The argument had ended by the time that all of the acrobats had disappeared. Marcus continued to snap shots of the clowns who had come forward to do one more dance. The clowns exited, except for the clown with the drum on her outfit. She had been on the floor the entire time helping to pick up some of the stray items such as balls that had gotten away from circus performers.

"That was hot!" said Marcus.

"Yeah, all that flipping! For a minute I thought that one of those acrobats was going to fall!" Havier added.

When the final clown with the drum on her outfit had exited the arena, the ring announcer broadcast the intermission.

"Want to get a hot dog?" asked Marcus.

"Aight," Havier replied.

The Wright brothers headed toward the hotdog stand. It was located outside of the seating arena. A long line had already formed.

"What are you getting? I'm getting a hotdog, popcorn, cotton candy and a soda," said Marcus.

"That's a waste of money," said the fiscally conservative Havier.

"Come on Havier, this is the Black circus. We don't go to the circus every day."

"The Black man will never get ahead spending all that money."

Marcus surprisingly countered his brother's point with a highly intelligent answer, but then ruined his argument by laughing at the end, "But it's for the Black circus. The Black circus is owned, operated and run by the Black man. I mean how many stores do we go to in Brooklyn and spend a lot more money? Plus, we don't even own them. Here's our chance, and I'm taking it!"

Despite the laughter at the end, Havier was taken aback by Marcus' proclamation. Havier offered a weak reply because of his embarrassment, "Marcus you are making sense now, but that's not just because you want that popcorn and cotton candy is it?"

"Nah," Marcus brushed it off. "You're getting a hotdog and a soda, right?"

Havier agreed grudgingly to buy the hotdog, "Yeah, but no popcorn or a cotton candy for me."

The Wright brother's turn was approaching. The total bill came to $23.45.

"That's a lot of money," said Marcus,

"That's what I was saying," Havier replied.

The intermission break was almost over. The Wrights headed back to their seats. Havier pointed their father's camera at the central arena and said, "I can't wait for the circus to begin to snap these shots!"

"Maybe you could let me hold the camera for a minute after the show starts," Marcus said to his older brother.

"You must be crazy. Never that, you got your turn. It's time for me to start snapping," Havier asserted to his brother.

The ring announcer came out and began to speak. However, something seemed strange because the lights were still on. There was no spot light on the ringmaster and he was not speaking in that usual, "Step right up!" circus voice. Instead, he spoke in a plain, somewhat humdrum tone, "Ladies and gentleman," he began, "I am sorry to have to bring you this news, but one of our Ethiopian acrobats is missing from the circus grounds. It appears as if she disappeared during the course of the grand finale just before intermission. In fact, she was the last acrobat to disappear during the magician's act. There is no need for panic; the police have been notified. If anyone saw anything suspicious, the police have set up a temporary substation in the east section of the arena next to the hotdog stand. You can also call the city's crime tips hotline or notify officers in your local precinct. As for the circus, it has been closed until further notice. Please be sure to pick up a voucher when you exit. You can exchange it for a future ticket."

"Check that out! This seems like some serious business," Marcus exclaimed.

"Yeah! To shut down the Black circus is serious business," Havier agreed.

The Wright brothers got up from their seats and headed for the arena exit.

"I can't believe that the acrobat just up and disappeared like that," said Havier.

"You think she ran away or something?" asked Marcus.

"In the middle of a show?" Havier questioned his brother's last statement. "If she had run away wouldn't she do it before or after the show?"

"Yeah, unless she wanted to hurt the show."

"Like she got beef with the show manager or something."

"Something like that," Marcus said sounding unsure.

The Wright brothers passed the hotdog stand and the police substation, and began to descend toward the exit.

"Yeah, but why would she have beef with the show manager?" asked Havier.

"Could be a lot of reasons. Maybe she was not flipping on the trapeze right and they got mad at her," Marcus explained unclearly.

"But you saw the acrobats and they had an excellent performance today."

"Maybe something else."

The hallways of the arena became so noisy that it was impossible to carry on a conversation. Therefore, the Wright brothers walked silently toward the exit. As they exited the door, they were handed their vouchers and left the arena. The young men walked to the subway stop and waited for the train on the elevated platform.

"I don't think the runaway idea is true," Havier stated.

"Huh?" Marcus questioned.

"The Ethiopian acrobat disappeared during the act. Plus the cops were called to find her. They had a station and everything."

"Well they could have set up the station even if she ran away,"

"True that, but she disappeared in front of ten thousand people. That just doesn't make sense. If she was running away, somebody would have seen her," said Havier.

A train approached and the Wright brothers entered and sat down. The doors closed and the train rumbled to the next stop.

"Somebody had to have seen her," said Marcus.

"Somebody did. You saw all those people going to the police substation," replied Havier.

"Yeah, I wish I saw something. This ruined my day. You know the circus closing and all. Plus that acrobat is probably someplace bad. Imagine if we saw who took her. We could solve the case for the police. Our pictures would be everywhere. We would be famous like the people Dad photographs," Marcus said in a dreamy tone of voice.

"That's it Marcus! The camera! You probably got the whole crime of the disappearing acrobat on film!" Havier exclaimed.

Havier frantically scrambled to take out the camera from its carrying case as the train screeched to another stop.

"You took seven hundred and forty-three pictures in one hour! That's about one picture every five seconds. You had to catch the disappearing acrobat on film!" Havier excitedly said to his brother.

Havier began to browse through the stored images.

"No not that one, not that one. No, not that. That's not it," Marcus said while looking over Havier's shoulder.

"Lucky this camera allows you to separate a section of the pictures!" said Havier.

"Yeah you could pull out all of the pictures on a separate hard drive," replied Marcus.

"Well it looks like there are eighty-seven pictures from the part of the show that the acrobat disappeared from," said Havier.

"Any luck in finding the one that she's missing from?" asked Marcus.

"Not yet. I think we better look at them on a bigger screen when we get home."

"You think we should bring it back to the five-o station in the circus arena?"

Havier looked up in deep thought, "Nah that doesn't make sense. We're almost home. Let's just check out these pictures on a bigger screen," Havier added.

"Yeah there might not be anything in those pictures anyway," Marcus added.

The train rumbled to the Wright brother's Brooklyn stop.

"Our stop came up so quick," said Havier.

"Yeah," Marcus agreed with his brother as they exited the train.

"Let's hurry home quick!"

"I can't wait to see them shots."

The Wright brothers walked quickly toward their brownstone and unlocked the door.

"Dad guess what happened at the circus?" Havier said enthusiastically entering his home.

"You seem very excited. What happened?" Mr. Wright responded.

"There was an Ethiopian acrobat who disappeared from the circus. The entire show was canceled, but we think Marcus may have taken a picture of the disappearance with the Supermaxtronic 3000 camera you lent us," Havier explained.

"I can't believe it!" Marcus added.

Mrs. Wright entered the room and said, "You guys sound pretty excited, but let's not forget that the acrobat could be in a dangerous situation."

"Right Mom, we have to take a closer look at the pictures to find out," said Havier.

"Wow a disappearance of one of the acrobats and a closure of the circus. That's something else! Well I'm not using the photo lab in the basement right now so you fellows can use the computers to take a better look at those images," their father said in a welcoming voice.

"Come on let's go," said Havier to Marcus.

"You don't have to ask me twice!" Marcus responded enthusiastically.

The Wright brothers went downstairs.

"Turn on the computer, I'll get the light," said Marcus.

The young men waited in anticipation as the computer booted up. The camera's extra pack contained ten hard drives. Each hard drive could hold hundreds of high resolution pictures. Marcus had set the camera to the highest resolution so he got some of the best images possible.

"I wish these pictures would load a little bit quicker," said Havier.

"Yeah, but at least they will be the highest quality. It took almost two of the hard drives to take the pictures. That means that each hard drive can hold about four hundred high resolution pictures."

The images loaded onto the computer one by one. After they were completed Havier isolated the eighty-seven pictures of interest on a separate file. He also made copies of them on several DVD's. They took up an entire spindle of DVD's. They also made a second copy of all of the pictures. This took awhile because they scaled down all of the pictures so that they took a lot less computer space. In fact, they were able to fit all of the pictures on only two DVD's.

"Making a backup is always important," said Havier.

"Yeah, remember that time Dad lost pictures of the mayor of New York City," Marcus added.

"That was bad."

"Now that copies are made let's get to work."

The Wright brothers browsed through the pictures of the magician, acrobats, clowns, trapezes, elephants, lions, tigers, trampolines, ringmaster and surrounding audience. Most of this section of eighty-seven pictures were relatively blurry. In fact some of the pictures were so blurry that it was not clear what was being photographed.

"That must have been when you were arguing with me about getting the camera and you made me shake it," said Marcus in an annoyed tone.

"Made you! You were holding the camera!" said Havier angrily.

"It looks like twenty-one, no twenty-two of the eighty-seven pictures are very blurry. Although some of them look a little better than others," Marcus observed who had been keeping track.

"The disappearance must have happened somewhere in these pictures. Between picture number forty-one and picture number sixty-two in this set of eighty-seven the disappearance most likely occurred. Look, the Ethiopian acrobat is right there in picture number forty," Havier zoomed in on her face with the computer. "Then the pictures become blurry and by picture number sixty-three, the acrobat no longer shows up in any of the remaining pictures."

"Yeah, its too bad pictures forty-one through sixty-two are too blurry to see anything," said Marcus. "But some of the earlier pictures in this set are also too blurry to see. Look at pictures number twenty-five through thirty-two. Those are very blurry too. And pictures seven through fifteen are also quite blurry."

"Well let's use the zoom feature and the clarity feature on the computer picture program before we come to any conclusions," explained Havier.

After much time trying, the Wright brothers found that the clarity and zoom features did not help much.

"The blurry spots of the photos aren't getting much better," said Marcus.

"Yeah it just looks like a bunch of blurry circus colors," said Havier.

"It looks like you can make out the horses and elephants in this picture."

"Yeah and there is a person but the wide angled shots are not clear as to who is who."

"We could figure out which person is which except that all of the acrobats have on the same colors."

"Let's call Dad. Maybe he can help," Marcus replied.

"Good idea," said Havier.

After much refinement of the pictures, Mr. Wright said, "Well boys, I can't do much better than you. The trampolines look a little bit clearer and you can make out the acrobats and clowns a little better. But you still can't see their faces. And without the faces, I don't know how you would be able to figure out what happened to the Ethiopian acrobat."

The police had a station in the circus arena. Do you think we should turn the pictures in to them?" asked Marcus.

"Yes you should. That's a good idea Marcus." replied Mr. Wright. "Go down to the local precinct and turn them into the Captain tomorrow."

"Ok, Dad!" said Marcus and Havier in tandem.

"Just be sure to save a copy of the pictures for yourself," Mr. Wright added.

"Yes sir. We already made a backup copy," said Marcus politely.

"Great!" Mr. Wright responded.

"The Wright brothers watched a little bit of television. They were so anxious to get to the precinct the next morning that they went to bed at 9:30pm.

Chapter 6: The Precinct

The Wright brothers woke up at 5:15am. They quickly got ready and walked over to the precinct. Upon their arrival, two Caucasian police officers sat behind a tall counter. One of them was large and the other man was skinny. The skinny man's eyes looked sleepy and the heavy officer was yawning. The heavyset cop stood up and walked through a door into a rear section of the precinct. He did not seem as though he was paying attention to anything.

Havier and Marcus approached the skinny officer and Havier spoke, "Excuse me sir, we have some information about the disappearance of the acrobat at the Black circus in the Bronx yesterday."

The skinny officer responded to Havier, "Wow that's a big case! It made the headlines in the papers this morning. Apparently it is being investigated by the department as a kidnapping. What kind of information do you have?"

"We have some pictures," Havier responded. "We were there taking some pictures."

The skinny officer motioned to Havier as he spoke, "I see. Come with me." He put his hand up in the air to stop Marcus who had stepped forward and said, "You stay here young man."

The skinny police officer allowed Havier to walk ahead of him as he opened the door that the heavyset officer had walked through. The officer and Havier disappeared as the door closed with an eerie thump behind them. The cop took Havier to a room and told him to sit down at a table.

"So where are the pictures?" asked the officer.

Havier handed him the DVD's containing the pictures.

"What did you say your name was and how old are you?"

Havier told the skinny officer his name and age.

"Hold on a second. I'll be right back," said the officer.

The skinny police officer disappeared and returned with a huge Caucasian officer who was twice as large as the heavyset officer he had seen up front.

The skinny officer introduced the heavyset officer, "Havier, this is Officer McNamara."

Officer McNamara had an angry look on his face as he said, "So Officer Thompson here says that you were at the circus and know about the acrobat's disappearance."

"Yes, well my brother and I were at the circus taking pictures and we thought it would help you solve the case if we gave them to you. Some of them aren't very clear, but we thought that it would be of help," explained Havier.

"Help! Help! Are you sure you boys aren't involved in this kidnapping?" Officer McNamara said raising his voice.

Havier was flabbergasted at the accusation, "No sir. I was just..."

Officer McNamara screamed, "Just what! About to tell me that you had something to do with it! That you know where that acrobat is!" He lowered his tone and said in a firm, yet angry voice, "I think you'd better think pretty hard about your involvement in the acrobat's disappearance."

Officer McNamara stormed out of the room. Officer Thompson reached in a paper bag that he had resting on the table.

"Here kid," he said compassionately handing him a soda. "I was going to have this soda for lunch, but you can have it."

"No thanks," Havier said as he realized that Officer Thompson's kindness was really a trick to get him to confess to something he hadn't done.

"Well here, have the soda anyway, Havier," Officer Thompson said pushing the soda across the table to Havier. "I'm going to leave you for a few minutes to think about the situation."

Havier had viewed this scene many times on television and in the movies. But it felt much different to be under the pressure of a hostile interrogation. These officers were making him feel like he had done something wrong.

In the meantime, Marcus had quickly become bored in the precinct waiting room. The heavyset cop had returned to the desk.

Marcus asked him a question that he had always wondered, "Excuse me sir, if someone breaks into your home to rob you and you have a registered gun and you shoot him in the back, is that considered illegal?"

The heavyset cop responded in a very hostile tone, "Why? Who did you shoot?"

Marcus felt awful after getting this response and he replied quickly, "No one sir."

"You sure?"

"Yes sir. I didn't shoot anyone," Marcus answered politely.

That ended that conversation for a few minutes. Marcus wondered when his brother would emerge from the precinct. He just wanted to go home. Then the door to the rear of the precinct swung open. Marcus' excitement quickly turned to disappointment. It was the skinny cop, the one that Havier had come to know as Officer Thompson.

"We want to talk to that kid," Thompson said while pointing at Marcus.

The heavyset officer sitting behind the desk commented, "He says he shot someone."

"No I didn't," Marcus said with a worried, defiant tone.

"Oh yeah? Shot someone?" Officer Thompson said skeptically.

"Yep, he shot the person in the back," the plump officer added.

"Oh, thanks," said Officer Thompson. "Young man, come with me."

Marcus followed him into a small room. Marcus was taken aback because Havier wasn't in the room.

"Have a seat. What's your name and how old are you?" Officer Thompson asked and Marcus told him his name and age. Then Officer Thompson walked out of the room. He went into the main office where Officer McNamara was doing some paperwork for another case.

"I think we should get the older one to confess to the kidnapping of the acrobat because he's sixteen. Then we can show the younger one the confession and get him to sign one too. Then once we've made the arrest, we can get the younger one to sign another confession saying that he shot someone else in a park and then use that to get the older one to confess to murder. I mean it'll go over smoothly in the media, courts and everything," said McNamara to Thompson.

"Ok sounds good to me," responded Officer Thompson. "I'll type the confessions."

After a few minutes, the two men entered the room where Havier was seated. Officer Thompson took a seat to the side of Havier in a programmed manner as if he had done it several thousand times before. He gave McNamara a nod.

Officer McNamara spoke in a cold, stern voice, "Look Havier, we know you did it. We know you kidnapped and hurt the acrobat in the process. Sign it and you'll be out in three years."

"Havier," Officer Thompson said in a much gentler tone, "if you sign the confession, I'll personally ask the judge to go easy on you. I'll ask him to give you two years. What do you say Havier?"

Fortunately, Havier was much more knowledgeable about the police's coercion of young Black men. This daily harassment was highlighted in a famous case back in the 1980's. The case involved several young Black teenagers who were forced in a similar manner to confess to a crime that another man committed. After serving their entire prison term, another man confessed to the crime and all of the evidence proved that he'd done it and that the teens did not. The entire youth of these men was destroyed by the forced false confessions elicited by the police.

Moreover, Havier knew that it is a jury or judge that makes the decision to lighten the sentence, not an officer of the law.

"Well young man, are you going to sign?" Officer Thompson asked.

"Oh he's going to sign! He's going to sign!" Officer McNamara screamed while bolting from the corner of the room, slamming his hand on the table and bending over to face Havier.

"Look Havier, it's hard for me to tell you this, but your brother Marcus just told me what happened. He said you and him kidnapped her from the circus. He also said he shot someone in the park and that he was the trigger man. Come on Havier let me help you out. Sign the confession and I'll get you two years," Officer Thompson said as sympathetically as he could.

Havier didn't want to say something that might get him in trouble. He was well aware of what police officers did to solicit false confessions. A false confession was when you confess to a crime that you did not commit. Havier had read articles about how police would even dress up like a criminal and enter a holding cell or jail to get a confession from an unsuspecting person. And the worst part of it was that it was legal. Most courts would allow these tricky confessions into evidence.

Havier kept repeating in his mind, "You have the right to remain silent, anything you say can and will be used against you in a court of law. Don't say anything. Just get out of here."

"But I didn't do anything," Havier blurted out.

"You better sign that paper because you're in a lot of hot water!" Officer McNamara yelled at the top of his lungs.

"Go ahead. Sign the paper," said Officer Thompson in an encouraging tone.

"I don't want to," Havier responded.

"Would you prefer confessing to me on videotape?" Officer Thompson asked.

"No," Havier said firmly.

"But your brother confessed already! And you're going down for at least twenty-five years if you don't sign this confession!" Officer McNamara screamed at the top of his lungs.

Havier was very nervous. His hands were shaking.

"Here have the soda kid. Just sign the paper and I'll take care of you," said Officer Thompson in a soothing voice.

Havier summoned all his strength and spoke with all of the wisdom and knowledge that he had gained from Black history and his studies of the law, "My final answer is no. And if I am being arrested, I would like to speak to a lawyer. If I am not being arrested, I would like to go home with my brother now."

Havier was well aware of his rights, but he was not sure how these two officers would react. Surprisingly, Officer McNamara left the room slamming the door on the way out.

Officer Thompson said with disappointment in his voice, "Ok you can go home. Come with me. Your brother is two rooms over."

Havier followed Officer Thompson down the hall to the interrogation room where Marcus was seated.

As they walked, Havier thought, "Wow, I can't believe that they let me go that easy. And most people my age would have confessed."

"Marcus, your brother is waiting on you to go," said Officer Thompson.

Havier caught a glimpse of Marcus' face and he smiled. Marcus returned the smile. The Wright brothers walked silently behind Officer Thompson. They exited the door to the front of the precinct and then through the doors to the outside.

On their way out Officer Thompson said, "If you boys have anymore information about that kidnapping, you make sure you come back here."

Havier waited until he was at least two blocks away from the precinct and then he questioned Marcus, "What did you tell them Marcus?"

"Nothing," responded Marcus.

"Nothing? Or did you tell them something?" Havier asked again.

"I told them my name and age, and then Officer Thompson left me in that room. When he returned, he was with you."

"You didn't confess to kidnapping or shooting someone? Did you?"

"Confess? Why would I confess? They were trying to pin something on me because I asked a question, but then you came to the room and we left."

"I knew it. Those cops told me you had confessed to kidnapping the acrobat and shooting someone," Havier said.

"No, I just asked the cop at the front desk a legal question and he brought me in the back. Did he really tell you that I confessed?"

"Yeah."

"Let's tell Dad," said Marcus.

"I feel that!" Havier exclaimed.

The Wright brothers hurried home. Havier explained the story to their father because he knew the most about what happened in the precinct.

"I'm going to the precinct now!" said Mr. Wright angrily.

"Be careful Dad. Those cops will do anything to get you to confess to any crime," Marcus warned.

"Don't worry sons. I am personally friends with Captain James. He is a high ranking officer in the police department and he is a Black man," Mr. Wright explained and grabbed a camera as he left.

Several officers were walking out of the precinct as Mr. Wright approached. He snapped a close up of all of them. After entering the precinct, Mr. Wright questioned the officer behind the tall counter. He was a different officer than those who had harassed his sons. It was 8:15am and the new shift began at 8:00am.

"May I please speak to Captain James," asked Mr. Wright.

"Captain James is busy right now. Maybe I can help you," said one of the officers sitting behind the desk.

"Please tell Captain James that his good friend Samuel Wright is here to see him on a very urgent matter," commanded Mr. Wright.

The officer waddled over to the door leading to the back of the precinct pulled it open and yelled, "Hey Farley, there's a guy out here—Wright. Says he's a friend of the Captain and wants to see him."

"Captain's busy," a voice answered from behind the door.

"That's what I told him, but he said it's important," said the officer up front.

"Give me a minute," answered the voice behind the door.

"Have a seat. The Captain will be out in a few minutes," said the officer.

A tall, well-built Black man soon emerged from the door. His hair was cropped neatly at the sides and on top. He was wearing a neatly pressed uniform and his shoes were carefully shined.

"Hey how's it been Samuel?" Captain James gave Mr. Wright an African handshake.

"I'm sorry I have to say this, but a couple of your officers harassed my sons early this morning," said Mr. Wright.

"That's disturbing. Where did it happen in the neighborhood?" Captain James inquired.

"No, it happened right here in the precinct. My sons came to turn in some pictures they took at the circus during the kidnapping of the Ethiopian acrobat, and two of your cops, Thompson and McNamara, took them in the back and tried to get them to sign a confession."

"A confession? That's very disturbing. I'm doing a house cleaning at this precinct right now. We have a lot of corrupt cops. I was aware of McNamara's shady ways, but Thompson? Hold on a second, let me check the evidence repository," he said and disappeared through the door.

The precinct had an eerie silence. Then Captain James returned to the front.

"Officer Thompson had filed these pictures on DVD's under his name. He says here in his notes that they were dropped off by an unidentified Caucasian witness."

"That can't be because I have an exact copy of all of those pictures at home. There was another officer too who also participated in the harassment of my sons. He was seated out front here," Mr. Wright explained.

"I know who that is and I will speak with him. In addition, I'm going to have a long talk with Officer Thompson and McNamara. They will be assigned to desk duty in the back until this investigation has been completed. No more arrests or interrogations for them, it's desk duty from now on and they will probably be fired."

"Well, you know this is a big news story. Something has got to be done about this. Sure, I can expose this to the press, but what about the young Black men that go through this on a daily basis who don't have influential fathers?"

"You make a very important point. Black men are more likely to be harassed by the police. We are more likely to be detained, accused, arrested and convicted. We are also more likely to receive poor legal representation.

But you know who the real criminals are. They are in high places of power. I'm trying to clean as much of it up as I can on a local level. I'm sorry for what happened to your sons and I would welcome a story in the paper. It would help me to get rid of those three corrupt cops as well as put the rest of the corrupt, racist officers on notice," Captain James affirmed.

"As soon as you catch the people who are responsible for the acrobat's disappearance, I'm going to release the story to the press," said Mr. Wright.

"Sounds good to me."

"I'll see you later," Mr. Wright said as he turned to leave the precinct.

"Take care," replied Captain James.

After arriving at home, Mr. Wright told his sons and wife what had happened.

"I want you two young men to know that you did the right thing. Those police officers were racist and corrupt, and Captain James is going to deal with them."

"I can't believe that they would do that to you. Samuel, I think that we should do something about this. Maybe we should contact one of the activists you know and organize a rally," Mrs. Wright said firmly.

"That's a good idea I'm going to have to consider that," Mr. Wright replied.

"Yes, we've got to do something Samuel. These are our sons being harassed by the police. We have to stand up and speak out."

"Well, after Captain James apprehends the people involved in the crime at the circus, I am going to release a story to the media, exposing the officers involved. I feel that this is the best way to show that these officers falsely accused Havier and Marcus of the crime."

"That's a good idea Samuel. Let the Captain catch the people who committed this crime. When all of the evidence is on the table, it will be pretty difficult to argue that they thought our sons had anything to do with it."

"Ok so that's what I'll do."

"Thanks Dad!" The Wright brothers exclaimed with relief.

The Wright family enjoyed the remaining time that Sunday together.

Chapter 7: Questions and More Questions

The week went by quickly. As the weekend approached the young men became refocused on the case. By Friday the acrobat had not been found, and the circus had not been reopened. It wasn't that the circus couldn't continue without the acrobat, but that the negative publicity that went along with reopening it was a risky business decision. Thus, the circus management decided upon a temporary cooling period until the acrobat was found. The Wright brothers watched the nightly news on television to see the coverage of the case of the disappearing acrobat.

As the news began, they watched intensely. The reporter announced, "While no further leads have been found in the case of the disappearing Ethiopian acrobat, the Black circus will reopen tomorrow. However, if the acrobat is not located during the next five weeks while the Circus is visiting New York, it will shut down indefinitely."

The news report switched to a scene of an African-American circus manager speaking. The circus manger had a deeply concerned look on his face. He was standing next to the African-American owner of the Black circus. The owner was an aged man who stared away from the camera with a tired expression. They were both wearing black tuxedos that were cleanly pressed.

As the circus manager spoke the Wright brothers could feel the intensity of the situation, "The Black circus was having a difficult time supporting itself without a major crisis like this. If the acrobat is not located, the circus will not tour other states this year and we will permanently shut it down."

The reporter concluded the story by saying, "Let's hope that the police find the acrobat soon."

"That's wack. No more Black circus. What would we do without the Black circus?" Marcus said in a worried tone to Havier.

"We would watch more rap videos with the big chains and diamond earrings; they're circus enough," Havier said teasing Marcus.

"No seriously Havier. I feel bad that the circus will be gone if the acrobat isn't found."

"Yeah, I know I'm just messing with you. I'm not trying to see the Black circus go either."

"Why don't we go to the circus tomorrow morning and ask some questions after the show?"

"I don't want to use my tickets until they find the acrobat. And even if we used the tickets, it's not like they would let us backstage to question the performers and managers. Besides, after what happened with the cops harassing us, I'm not trying to get caught up in that mess," Havier stated.

"What if we asked Dad for media passes? Sometimes he gets them for his assistants. They would let us in and we could ask whoever we wanted, whatever we wanted. Dad said he was going to write a story about them cops and what they did to us. Just imagine how much help it would be if he could explain the details about the circus performers, their names and what they do. I bet he would give us the passes," Marcus argued.

A smile came to Havier's face.

"I'm feeling that. Let's ask Dad at dinner."

"Aight," replied Marcus.

It was about one hour before Mr. and Mrs. Wright came home from work. They prepared dinner together and asked their two sons to help set the table and to prepare dinner. Their mother was making mashed potatoes and asked Havier and Marcus to help peel them.

"How was your day boys?" Mrs. Wright asked.

"Ok but there's still no word on the missing acrobat," said Havier.

"Really?" queried Mrs. Wright.

"Yes, but the circus is going to reopen tomorrow. The only problem is that the owner said that he is going to cancel it for good if the Ethiopian acrobat isn't found," Marcus worried out loud.

"For good!" Havier added with emphasis.

"That's something else," said Mrs. Wright.

"Yeah, canceling the Black circus sounds like a big deal," Mr. Wright added.

"Yeah Dad and we were thinking that…" Marcus paused.

"What were you thinking?" Mr. Wright sternly asked.

"Well...we were wondering if it would be possible to go back to the circus tomorrow and find out what the circus performers know about the case," Marcus asked with some hesitation in his voice.

"You two don't have a way to get back stage at the circus. Sure you can go, but I don't know how you are going to get into the circus without tickets or permission to go backstage," Mr. Wright explained.

"Well, we were wondering if it would be possible for you to give us temporary media passes? We thought that if we could interview the circus performers, the information could be used in your story on the precinct and to help the police solve the case," said Havier.

Addressing her husband Mrs. Wright said, "Wow that's really amazing that they want to help you and the police with their work. It's not often that you have two young men so motivated to help accomplish a task. Why not give them a shot?"

"So, I have two budding reporters as sons, who are also detectives in training. Well, to be a reporter you also have to be a detective. I just don't want you boys to impede the police investigation. You can have the media passes, but I'm going to notify Captain James that you fellows will be helping me with my story and that you will be asking questions at the circus. If you have any trouble, or if you get harassed, you call me right away," Mr. Wright said in a caring tone.

"Thanks Dad!" the Wright brothers said simultaneously.

"We'll be headed up there first thing in the morning," Marcus added.

"Ok let me write those media passes out for you now," said Mr. Wright who stood up, walked over to his briefcase, opened it and took out two temporary media passes. Mr. Wright worked with several prominent people in the media who had given him access to the passes. "Let's see. The circus is in town for five more weekends; so I will make the passes out to cover all of its performances. You two might want to go back again and ask more questions," said Mr. Wright.

"Thanks Dad," said Havier.

"Make sure that you call me if you need me and I will get in contact with Captain James right away," said Mr. Wright.

"We will," Marcus replied.

The Wright brothers left the table and wished their parents a good night. Then they did some reading and homework before they went to bed.

"If we go in the morning, we will have to wait until the show is over to interview the performers," said Havier.

"I want to see the Black circus again," said Marcus.

"Aight."

The following morning the Wright brothers woke up early and headed out. The train ride was rather boring and circus attendance was sparse.

"I guess people didn't want to buy tickets," said Marcus.

"Yeah they must have been too scared that something bad was going to happen again," added Havier.

The ring announcer began the show and the lights dimmed. Havier took out a small digital camera to take some pictures. The first half of the show was the same as before, but there was no magician shooting huge puffs of smoke in the air. That meant that none of the acrobats were disappearing. Instead, they just flew from trapeze to trapeze and occasionally bounced on two of the trampolines that were left in the arena. The Wright brothers were sad that the acrobat was missing from the performance.

The second half of the show seemed like more of the same to the Wright brothers. The missing acrobat and absence of the magician put them in a humdrum mood. As the show neared its end the two young detectives became more anxious to use their media passes to interview the circus performers.

"Come on let's go," Marcus said when the show was almost over.

"Aight," Havier agreed.

The Wright brothers headed to the lower tier of the circus arena. They flashed their media passes and were led into the back by two security guards. When the show concluded they interviewed all of the acrobats and clowns. They also spoke to two of the circus managers in the management office. They took careful notes even though most of the people that they spoke to did not provide useful information. Almost all of them expressed their concern for the missing Ethiopian acrobat named Zauditu. However, a few of the performers seemed to be suspicious while others offered an extensive amount of information. Two of them, Ralph the Magnificent Magician and Jake the Animal trainer caught the Wright brothers' attention. They were both African-American men. One of the Ethiopian acrobats, who had an assumed American name: Mary, and two African-American clowns Eric and Kia also piqued the Wright brother's interest.

When the Wrights spoke to Mary she seemed to answer questions in a strange manner.

"Did you see the acrobat disappear?" Havier asked her.

"One sees what he wants to in this world. We see only what we want to," answered Mary with an estranged look.

"But what about the acrobat, did you see where she disappeared to?" Marcus attempted to get her to answer.

"A vision of mine is to see all one day. I see only what I am allowed."

"But what about the acrobat. Did you see her disappear?" Havier asked again.

"She was great swinging from the trapezes. She was truly one of the greatest this circus had ever seen. When she was with us she was grand," Mary replied with vague responses.

"Thanks," said Havier.

Mary stared into space.

The two clowns of interest, Kia and Eric were much clearer with their answers than Mary.

"Nice to meet you, my name's Eric," the clown introduced himself while shaking Havier's hand.

"Nice to meet you, too," replied Havier.

"So how can I help you two young men?" Eric asked.

"Did you see the acrobat disappear?" asked Havier.

"I think we all saw her disappear. The question that I think you're trying to ask is if I know where she reappeared. Unfortunately, I don't have an answer to that question. I do know that you should probably ask the magician some questions. He would know how he made the acrobat disappear. He might know a lot more about the disappearance of the acrobat than you might think. A lot more."

"What about Mary, the acrobat. Do you think she was involved?" Havier asked.

"No way. That was one of her closest friends in the circus. She's just greatly disturbed about the loss of her friend. Unless you believe that foul play runs between friends," Eric laughed while saying this.

This made the Wright brothers unsure of whether he was telling the truth or laughing to cover up something.

"Thanks, sir," said Havier.

After Eric, the Wright brothers spoke to Kia.

"Pleased to meet you," said Kia.

"Nice to meet you too. My name's Havier and this is my brother Marcus.

"Kia's the name," she said with a smile.

"Did you see anything suspicious when the acrobat disappeared?"

"Do you mean Zauditu the Ethiopian acrobat who was kidnapped?" asked Kia.

"Yes ma'am," said Marcus

"Well all I know is that her friend Mary is acting kind of weird. You know they say that when someone talks about someone else in the past tense that they killed them. And that's how Mary talks about Zauditu. Ralph, the magician doesn't seem too right either. It was his magic that made her disappear. Why can't he bring her back? And then there is Jake the animal trainer. He seems pretty sneaky. And he was backstage during Zauditu's disappearance. He's the perfect candidate for the criminal act," said Kia.

"Thanks, Kia," said Havier.

"I think we'd better speak to Ralph the Magnificent Magician," Marcus added.

As they approached the magician's tent they heard a voice say, "Come into my tent young men."

This was somewhat frightening because the tent was closed and it was impossible to see into or out of it. Moreover, when they entered the tent, Ralph the Magnificent Magician was standing all the way at the rear.

"Hi I'm Havier Wright and this is my brother..." said Havier as he was interrupted. Being interrupted made Havier less focused upon the reason they were there. As he tried to recompose himself, the magician spoke.

"Hold on don't tell me, your name starts with an 'M' right?" the magician asked in a commanding tone.

"How did you know that?" Marcus inquired.

"Let's see, Ma, Ma, Marcus is your name," said Ralph.

"Wow!" Marcus exclaimed.

"My name is Ralph, the Magnificent Magician," the man explained as he approached the Wright brothers.

"Could we ask some questions about Zauditu?" asked Marcus.

"Sure, she was the acrobat who disappeared into thin air," Ralph replied.

"Yes but wasn't it you who made her disappear?" asked Marcus.

"Things aren't always what they seem young man," Ralph said trying to evade their question.

"Then how did you make the acrobats disappear in a puff of smoke?" asked Havier.

"Why, you would have to attend magic school to discover that young man. A good magician never reveals his trick," said Ralph.

"But this is a criminal investigation sir," Marcus tried to assert himself in a firm tone.

"And I spoke to the police," said the magician. He continued, "I will leave you with a riddle:

"It is the first cloud
That rings the ear
A blast, a saunter
But only with the second one reappears
A clue might lie in he who sits
Two thousand twenty-seven two-fifth."

At that, Ralph the Magician waved his wand and was consumed by a large cloud of smoke. About one or two seconds passed, the smoke cleared and the Wright brothers didn't see him anywhere. Then they heard the Magician laughing incessantly.

"Ha, ha, ha, ha," the laughter echoed in the tent.

The Wright brothers could not determine the direction of the laughter. Then another puff of smoke appeared near the desk at the rear of the tent and Ralph the Magnificent Magician appeared sitting at the desk with a sealed pad of paper in his hands. He rose from his seat behind the desk, ripped off the plastic and handed the pad of paper to Havier.

Havier read it aloud:

"It is the first cloud
That rings the ear
A blast, a saunter
But only with the second one reappears
A clue might lie in he who sits
Two thousand twenty-seven two-fifth."

"That was hot!" said Marcus somewhat mesmerized.

"We still have to speak to other people. Thank you for your time," said Havier who was somewhat annoyed.

Upon exiting Ralph's tent, Havier said in a very low whisper, "I don't trust that guy at all."

Marcus nodded because he was afraid to say anything.

The Wright brothers entered the tent that read, "Animal Training Area." Sure enough, a man was grooming one of the horses.

"Are you Jake the animal trainer?" asked Havier.

"Yes, Jake's the name and you are?"

"I'm Havier and this is my brother Marcus. We were wondering what you knew about Zauditu's disappearance," Havier inquired.

"Nothing much. Ralph the magician made her disappear and he can't make her reappear," said Jake.

"Are you sure that's what happened?" asked Marcus.

"Am I sure? Questions, questions. Got to go to Ultracut," said Jake.

He abruptly stopped grooming the horse and hurriedly disappeared out of the rear of the tent.

"So much for getting information out of him," said Havier.

"Yeah," agreed Marcus.

"Well, he was the last person we had to speak to. So I guess we can head home."

"Yeah, let's be out."

Nothing happened on the train ride home with the exception of the man selling M&M's.

"Not one M&M, not two M&M's but three juicy delicious M&M's for one dollar!" the man announced throughout the subway car.

When the Wright brothers got home they shared what they had learned with their parents and went to sleep.

Chapter 8: Guilty Acts

The Wright brothers awoke that Sunday morning feeling refreshed.

"Who do you think did it?" asked Marcus

"I don't know. Any one of them could have done it," said Havier.

"That elephant trainer is type guilty," said Marcus.

"Yeah, we asked him one question and he was ghost."

"Why would he run? Unless he just had something to do at that time."

"And you know he didn't have nothing to do because he was in the middle of taking care of that horse. He was combing it for the next show."

"Yeah and you can't just groom a horse in five minutes. Plus he left the horse half uncombed," Havier replied.

"I know it was him, I just can't prove it," Marcus affirmed.

"But what about Mary?"

"She seemed in a daze," Marcus replied.

"But she was the closest person in the circus to Zauditu."

"That's why she was in a daze because she lost her friend."

"True that. But what about Eric the clown? He could have done it right?"

"Nah, Eric was straight forward and honest."

"Except for that laugh; except for that laugh. Sometimes those that seem least guilty are those who are the most guilty."

"But Ralph the magician had a laugh too. Plus he had all them tricks. I don't trust him at all," Marcus stated.

"And that riddle, what's that supposed to mean?" Havier asked.

"I'll tell you what it means. It means he had a role in doing it. He did it and he probably had help from Jake the animal trainer," Marcus affirmed.

"Let's not jump to conclusions too quickly. The truth is that any of them could have done it. Sure, I think that Jake and Ralph are pretty suspicious, but so is Mary. And I wouldn't leave Eric out of the picture either, because he tried to point the finger at Ralph," Havier warned his younger brother.

"So the question is: Where should we start?"

"Good question. I'm not sure."

"Let's go check out what Ultracut is. That's where Jake said he was headed yesterday. It sounds like a barbershop. Maybe someone there knows something about his role in the crime."

"Let's find out," Havier said picking up the phone and dialing information. "The Bronx, New York. Ultracut please; it's a business," he told the operator.

Havier wrote down the number, hung up the phone and began to dial the number. A machine came on, "This is Ultracut where the cut is always smooth. We are located between One Hundred Seventieth and One Hundred Seventy-First street just off the Grand Concourse. We are open everyday starting at 11:00am, but we have a Sunday morning special. Get that cut before you go to church; we're open at 8:30am on Sunday." Then the message gave the address to the barbershop and repeated itself.

We're in luck," said Havier, "they open at 8:30am today."

"What time is it now?" asked Marcus.

Both brothers simultaneously glanced at the clock on the living room wall.

"It's 8:00," said Havier.

"Let's be out," said Marcus.

"Aight."

The Wright brothers quickly got ready. Marcus had recently purchased a cubic zirconium earring and put it into his pierced ear. After he got it in he stood tall; admiring himself in the mirror. Havier looked over at him and gave him a disgruntled look. Nevertheless, he did not say anything about Marcus' earring. He had made himself loud and clear on this subject many times and had decided not to say anymore to his brother. However, Havier's stare alone was enough to send a clear and loud message of disapproval. As a result, Marcus hung his head a little bit lower, and didn't feel so proud to have his fake diamond earring in.

When this uncomfortable moment had ended, they headed down to the train. It was about 8:30am when they got there. They waited for the train for some time and made it to the barbershop by 9:55am. For at least fifteen minutes the Wrights debated how they were going to approach the situation. Then they resolved the debate.

"I'll ask about Jake," said Havier.

"You usually speak first when we go somewhere," replied Marcus.

"That's because I'm afraid you will say something you're not supposed to."

"But sometimes that helps us."

"And sometimes it hurts us too. But if you want to speak first this time, I guess that's ok," Havier countered.

"Nah, that's all right. You speak first," Marcus conceded.

With this common understanding, the two detectives entered the barbershop.

"Looking for the Sunday morning special?" One of the barbers closer to the front of the store said yawning.

"Actually, we wanted to speak to someone about Jake from the Black circus," said Havier.

"Who are you?" the barber responded in a dreary tone.

"We're investigating the case of the disappearing acrobat and we had some questions," Havier explained.

"Oh really?" the barber said in a sarcastic tone. "Speak to him," the barber pointed with his head to the tallest barber in the back. "He cuts Jake's hair."

The Wright brothers walked to the back of the store to the tall barber.

"How you doing little man?" the tall barber asked Havier in a deep voice.

"Ok, I guess," said Havier who wasn't used to being called little.

"So you need some info about Jake?" said the tall barber.

"Yeah," replied Havier.

"Well, he came in yesterday for a shape up. He always comes to this barbershop when the Black circus is in town. Jake's real cheap. He never tips at all and sometimes pays for his haircuts with quarters, dimes and nickels. One time he tried to pay me with pennies, but I told him we don't take pennies. It took him two weeks before he finally paid me. He said the circus hadn't paid him yet," the tall barber commented. "Anyway, he comes in late yesterday and asks for a shape up. But he kept talking strange talk," said the tall barber.

"What did he say?" asked Havier.

"Something about he didn't do it. That's all he kept muttering was that he didn't do it. And that he 'aint confessing to nothing especially to no little thugs. You two wouldn't happen to be the two little thugs he was talking about?" said the tall barber.

"No, we're detectives not thugs," replied Marcus.

"Well anyway, Jake came in here saying he didn't do it. Then he raced out of here before I could finish his shapeup, and he said he would come back today. That's the strangest I've ever seen Jake act," said the tall barber.

"For real?" asked Havier.

"It's as true as my shoe!" the tall barber exclaimed. "He's supposed to be back at 10:30 this morning. Maybe if you wait around, he would speak to you, but I bet he's coming late."

"Thanks," said Havier.

It was 10:19am. Havier and Marcus decided to wait until Jake came. They stepped outside to wait for him. Sure enough, he was late. He came walking hurriedly down the street at 10:47am. When he saw Havier and Marcus, he stopped abruptly and stared at them. He was standing about one hundred feet away.

The stare down continued for some time.

All of a sudden Jake screamed, "Leave me be!"

Havier started to walk toward Jake and Marcus followed.

"We just wanted to ask you a few questions," said Havier

"I didn't have a part in it! I'm not guilty!" Jake yelled as he took off running in the opposite direction.

Marcus ran after him.

"Wait, Marcus, we don't have any evidence against him!" Havier said trying to stop his brother. However, Marcus kept running, so Havier followed.

Jake ran down a side street toward Jerome Avenue. The Wright brothers followed close behind him. Jake was fast, but the two young detectives were catching up to him.

"Stop!" Marcus shouted.

Jake started to climb a fence that was blocking an alleyway between two buildings. The fence had barbed wire at the top.

"We got him now! He's not going to make it over that fence without getting caught on the barbed wire!" Marcus yelled.

Jake threw up one foot on the barbed wire. It wasn't that razor wire that is on many Bronx fences. Instead, it was ordinary barbed wire containing three equally spaced, horizontal strands of wire with twisted metal barbs along each of the strands. Jake pushed the wire as far down as he could with his right foot as the Wright brothers approached the fence. He kicked his left foot in the air, did a three hundred sixty degree spin, and flipped over the fence.

"Ah!" he screamed as his left arm caught a barb on the way down. Jake landed on the ground, kept running and disappeared at the end of the alleyway between the two buildings.

"I can't believe that he was able to jump over that fence so easily!" Havier exclaimed.

"I can't believe we lost him," Marcus added with a hint of disgust in his voice.

"How'd he fly over that fence?"

"I don't know, but I do know he did it. He is responsible for Zauditu's disappearance. I know it."

"I think so too. But then again there are other suspects to consider," replied Havier.

"Can't you see that he's mad guilty," Marcus said as he started to get annoyed.

"Like I said, I think so too, but it's not good to jump to conclusions like that. It could've been any of the suspects. I'm not ruling out Ralph the magician."

"But Jake practically said he did it."

"Not exactly and we can't close any doors on our investigation," Havier answered patiently.

The Wright brothers walked silently back toward the barbershop.

Then Havier spoke, "Where are we going? Shouldn't we be headed home?"

"Yeah, let's be out," said Marcus.

The Wright brothers headed in the opposite direction and walked away from the barbershop and toward the train. They waited for the train and rode it all the way back to Brooklyn. When they got home it was 12:33pm.

Chapter 9: The Magician's Riddle

"So where do we go from here?" Marcus asked.

"Well it doesn't look like we are going to get another word out of Jake. And Mary and Eric weren't too helpful, but we do have the riddle from Ralph the magician. Here it is," Havier said pulling it out of his pocket. "I think that it's a good starting point." Havier read the paper out loud:

"It is the first cloud
That rings the ear
A blast, a saunter
But only with the second one reappears
A clue might lie in he who sits
Two thousand twenty-seven two-fifth."

"What in the world does that mean?" Marcus said in a confused tone.

"Well, let's break it down. The first part is about the clouds. I think it means that when he does that smoke trick that the first one makes himself or the acrobat disappear. Then on the second blast the acrobat or he reappears," Havier thought out loud.

"But what did he mean by 'a saunter?'"

"I don't know. What does saunter mean? Let's look it up," said Havier who reached for a dictionary off of the living room couch.

"So what does it mean Havier?"

"It means to stroll, walk or wander. Ah, I see. So that's what Ralph did between puffs of smoke. He hid behind the desk in his tent, created another puff of smoke and reappeared. The only thing is he must have been jetting not just walking because he got there real quick."

"So he gave away his trick. We know how he made Zauditu disappear," Marcus concluded.

"Not exactly, even if we know how he made people disappear, that does not explain where the acrobats on the circus floor went. Plus it doesn't explain how they magically reappeared on trampolines that were placed all the way on the other side of the circus arena. And it doesn't explain how Zauditu disappeared and didn't reappear," Havier explained.

"That's easy enough. She didn't reappear because there must not have been a second puff."

"But that would have meant that he was in on the kidnapping. And I know that's not what he meant to tell us with that riddle."

"You never know with these psychos out here."

"Well since we aren't sure whether he was talking about the acrobat or himself, then maybe we should table it for now and focus upon the second part of the riddle," Havier replied.

"We're supposed to find a man who's sitting somewhere and he can give us a clue," said Marcus.

"But what do the numbers mean?"

"I'm not sure. Maybe we should ask Mr. Billings.

"I think it's a street address," said Havier.

"In what borough, Manhattan, the Bronx, Queens, Brooklyn or Staten Island and what kind of street address is written like that?"

"That's a good question. Two-fifths is a fraction so it could be anywhere. I don't know of any streets that are fractions. He could have meant Second Street or Fifth Street. Or maybe he meant some other type of street. I don't think there's a Second or Fifth Street in the Bronx because all of the street numbers in the Bronx are over one hundred, and we've only been out to Staten Island a few times. So I'm not sure what's out there. But it could be in lower Manhattan, Brooklyn or Queens. I think all three of those boroughs have low numbered streets," Havier explained.

"Maybe we should ask Mr. Billings," Marcus thought.

"Good idea. He's got to be in the park."

"Yeah, he always takes walks in the park on Sunday afternoon. Let's be out." The Wrights left their home and headed over to the local park. Sure enough Mr. Billings was strolling through the park.

"Hey Mr. Billings, we have a problem," Havier began the conversation.

"How can I help?" Mr. Billings asked.

"Well, we're trying to locate the acrobat who disappeared from the Black circus. We have a clue, but don't know what it means. Havier took out the paper and read the second half of the riddle: 'A clue might lie in he who sits Two thousand twenty-seven two-fifth.'"

"Oh that's Mr. Collin's spot on One Hundred Twenty-Fifth Street in Harlem," said Mr. Billings without much thought.

"How do you know Mr. Billings? The paper says two-fifth, not One Hundred Twenty-Fifth Street," Marcus asked.

"It was a Black man who gave it to you right?" asked Mr. Billings.

"Yes sir. His name is Ralph the Magnificent Magician," said Marcus.

"Well I've never heard of him before, but many residents in Harlem truncate the "1" off of the street number. Therefore, they say twenty-fifth or two-fifth for One Hundred Twenty-Fifth Street, thirty-fifth for One Hundred Thirty-Fifth Street, and forty-fifth for One Hundred Forty-Fifth street. If there's something you want to know about Harlem or the Bronx, Mr. Collins knows it. That must be why you got that clue."

"Who would've guessed?" said Marcus.

"I'll tell you what to do. Just take the train to One Hundred Twenty-Fifth Street and walk down till you see storefront number two thousand twenty-seven. It's an old furniture shop. Mr. Collins will be sitting in front of the store. You can mention my name if you want."

"Thanks for the help, Mr. Billings," said Havier.

"Yeah, thanks for all the useful information," Marcus added.

The Wright brothers returned home, grabbed a camera and their temporary media passes. Then they were ready to try to find Mr. Collins on One Hundred Twenty-Fifth Street.

"Let's be out to Two-Fifth," said Havier.

"Aight," replied Marcus.

The ride to Harlem seemed much shorter than the ride to the Black circus in the Bronx even though One Hundred Twenty-Fifth Street is only a few stops away from the Bronx. The Wright brothers exited the train and walked down One Hundred Twenty-Fifth Street until they got to an antique store. It's address read, "2027." Sure enough, an elderly man was sitting in front of the store reading a book.

"Hello, young men," the man greeted the Wright brothers as they approached.

"Hello, sir," said Havier.

"Came for some antiques today?" asked the man.

"Actually," Marcus began to speak, "We were hoping to speak to Mr. Collins. Mr. Billings in Brooklyn sent us."

"I'm Mr. Collins. Mr. Billings is a good friend of mine. How can I help you two young men?"

"Have you heard of the Black circus?" said Havier.

"Do I know the Black circus? Do I know the Black circus? Why of course I know the Black circus," said Mr. Collins in a repetitive, yet confident manner.

"Well we're trying to solve a crime. Actually it's a disappearance…" Havier was interrupted by Mr. Collins.

"You're not talking about the Ethiopian acrobat Zauditu?"

"Yes sir. How did you know her name? None of the newspapers or television news reports have told the public her name," Marcus said curiously.

"I make it my business to know as much as I can about Black folk. Did you know that a famous woman in Ethiopia went by the name of Zauditu?" said Mr. Collins.

"Really?" responded Havier.

"Yes and she was the ruler of Ethiopia before Haile Selassie, also know as Rastafari, took the throne. Halie Selassie was a great leader you know. Ethiopia and Liberia were the only two African nations that were not fully colonized by Europeans and he was the head of one of them. Rastafarians all over the world revere him. You know I saw him when he made his address to the United Nations back in the 1960's. I also spoke to him for a brief while on the streets of New York City. He was really something else! Anyway how can I help you find out what happened to the acrobat Zauditu?"

"Well we got this riddle from Ralph the magician. We figured it out with Mr. Billings' help and it led to you," Havier explained.

"I know Ralph the Magnificent Magician. He's always with some pun. He's always trying to make a joke out of this or that. So he gave you some riddle leading to me huh?"

"Yes sir," replied Marcus.

"Well here's what I would say about all of this mess. That's what it is, a mess. A mess, I'll tell you…" Mr. Collins paused. "Where you should start is not with those circus performers. You need to take a look at how things are happening and how they happened while people's hands were clapping. You should look at the time, place, date, colors, shapes, sizes, height, width and all that jazzy stuff. Get it? Did I say enough? That's how you solve the crime. You fellows are smart; it's all sublime. Just use your mind and you'll solve the crime," said Mr. Collins.

Havier and Marcus began to wonder why Mr. Billings had sent them to Harlem to speak with Mr. Collins. It seemed as though Mr. Collins was aimlessly throwing out random, unrelated information in this conversation. He also seemed to be rhyming whenever he could just for the sake of rhyming. One of the only things that kept Havier and Marcus standing there was Mr. Collins' knowledge of the acrobat's name Zauditu. No one would know that unless they had taken the time to know many of the intimate details of the circus. Additionally, it seemed as though Mr. Collins also knew a lot about Ralph.

"Mr. Collins," Havier said in a measured tone.

"Yes, son?" Mr. Collins replied.

"Can you suggest a starting place for our investigation," Havier tried to sound as polite as he could, "I mean a real place that we can go to find out some sort of clue."

"If you want to go somewhere then you can start at *Party Hardy Now and Circus Enterprises*," said Mr. Collins with a serious face.

"Where's that located?" asked Havier.

"It's a store in downtown Manhattan," Mr. Collins said as he wrote down the address. "They sell circus and party supplies. They sell balloons, magic supplies, animal trainer supplies, new trapezes in case they break, trampolines, drums, flutes, guitars, horns, costumes, hats, shoes, ornamental jewelry and a whole bunch of other stuff. They sell everything but the kitchen sink, and they'll probably sell you one if you ask. All the circuses that come through New York City get most of their supplies there. Now when you go in there ask for Billy. Billy works in inventory. He works the late shift on Sunday afternoons, so you should be able to catch him today. Remember, 'Billy' and tell him that Mr. Collins sent you. He'll help you with whatever you need," said Mr. Collins.

"Thanks, Mr. Collins," said Havier.

"No problem young man. And you fellows be careful with them circus images that you took with your father's Supermaxtronic 3000 digital camera," Mr. Collins told the two young detectives.

"How did you know about the camera and pictures we took with it?" asked Marcus, who was shocked because only his father knew the type of camera that he had used to take the pictures at the circus. Even Captain James did not know what type of camera was used or that Mr. Wright even owned a Supermaxtronic 3000 camera.

"Mr. Collins knows. Mr. Collins makes sure he knows as much about his community as he can," said Mr. Collins wisely.

"See you later," said Marcus.

"That was hot! How did he know that we used Dad's Supermaxtronic 3000 digital camera to take pictures at the circus? We didn't even tell Mr. Billings about the camera or pictures," Havier exclaimed when they were far enough away.

"For real! Mr. Collins was off the hook! But he seemed so connected. Go figure." Marcus replied.

The ride to the circus supply store was short. The supply store occupied five floors in a building.

"This place is huge!" exclaimed Marcus.

"Yeah," Havier agreed.

"Excuse me sir, do you know where I could speak to a manager?" Havier asked an employee.

"An assistant manager is right over there," the employee said pointing to a gentleman who was about thirty years old.

"Excuse me sir," said Marcus in an excited tone. "Do you know anything about the Black circus performers. You know, we are detectives trying to track down the person responsible for the disappearance of the acrobat from the circus. It's actually a really exciting case and…"

"Well," the assistant manager interrupted Marcus, "The Black circus has a contract with us, but I can't give you anymore information than that," he said laughing at Marcus.

"That man thought I was a joke!" Marcus said in an angry tone to his older brother.

The Wright brothers walked away from the assistant manager.

"Mr. Collins told us to ask for Billy," Havier instructed his younger brother.

"Oh, yeah," remembered Marcus.

The Wright brothers strolled casually to another part of the store.

"Excuse me do you know where Billy is?" Havier asked an employee.

"Billy? There's no Billy who works here," the employee paused for a minute, "Hold on, do you mean William Brunson?" asked the employee.

"I guess," replied Havier sounding unsure.

"Well Mr. Brunson is the only person we have that would fit the name Bill or Billy. He's on the fourth floor towards the back of the building. You'll see him behind a tall counter," the employee explained.

The Wright brothers decided to take the stairs. They climbed the steep, wooden stairs which creaked with every step. When they made it to the fourth floor, both detectives were breathing heavy as they walked to the rear of the store where a young man in his early twenties sat behind a countertop.

"Excuse me sir are you Billy? I mean are you Mr. Brunson?" asked Marcus.

"You mean the inventory manager?" asked the young man.

"I'm Mr. Brunson," a man in his mid fifties said coming out of a door behind the counter.

"Hello sir, Mr. Collins sent us," said Havier.

"That explains why you called me Billy. That's what Mr. Collins called me when I was a child," said Mr. Brunson.

"You knew Mr. Collins that long?" asked Marcus.

"We grew up in the same Harlem community. Except, he was a young adult when I was about five years old. That's why I call him Mr. Collins and he calls me Billy," Mr. Brunson explained.

"Really?" Havier responded.

"Yes, but how is it that I can help you two young men?" asked Mr. Brunson.

"Do you know the case of the acrobat who disappeared from the circus?" asked Havier.

"Yeah, I know Zauditu. She came into this store on a few occasions when the circus was in town last year to pick up various extra items that had been ordered."

"Well we're trying to solve the case and Mr. Collins thought you would be able to help us," said Marcus.

"Unfortunately, I don't have any information about Zauditu's disappearance. She seemed like a nice person when she came into the store, but so do most of the circus performers. Maybe I could help you two young detectives by giving you a list of circus supplies that were ordered by the Black circus," said Mr. Brunson in a helpful tone.

"That would be great," said Havier to Mr. Brunson.

"Here is the inventory for the Black circus. They charge everything to one account so it makes things simple. When a performer wants an item, they just order it and the Black circus covers the bill. I'll leave you fellows a copy of the list. Each item has a number. If you want to see what an item looks like, just look for the item number on the shelf. They're stocked in numerical order on the shelves."

"Thanks Mr. Brunson," said Havier.

Havier and Marcus stared at the list for a moment. Then Havier began to flip through the list.

"Wow that list is real long," said Marcus.

"That's right. The circus orders hundreds of different types of circus items from us," Mr. Brunson replied.

The Wright brothers began to look at some of the items on the list and to locate them on the shelf.

After a few minutes, Havier looked up and down the list and said, "This is going to take a long time to look through all of the items. It might even take several visits to this store to go through all of them." Then Havier turned to Mr. Brunson and said, "Do you mind if we come back, Mr. Brunson?"

"Sure you can come back any time."

"Thanks," said Marcus.

The young men left the circus store and boarded the train. Upon arriving at their home they felt confident that they were on the trail of the person or people that were responsible for Zauditu's disappearance.

"I'm glad Mr. Collins gave us the info on that circus spot," said Marcus as the two brothers sat down in their living room.

"Yeah," Havier replied.

At that moment, Mr. Wright came in and said, "How are you fellows doing on the case?"

"We had an adventure packed weekend Dad," said Havier.

Marcus went on to explain all of the details of their weekend.

When Marcus was done speaking Mr. Wright said, "You fellows be sure to be careful. Remember, this is a kidnapper and potentially, well…" Mr. Wright paused for a minute.

"Potentially what Dad?" Marcus asked with a worried, inquisitive tone.

"Let's just hope that nothing happened to the acrobat," said Mr. Wright.

The Wright brothers got the point.

Chapter 10: A Physical Clue

The school week passed quickly for the Wright brothers. Surprisingly, the case had not distracted them from their class work. In fact, it had only enhanced their desire to learn. Most of all, Marcus stayed up late into the night doing his assignments so that he and Havier could spend as much time as possible solving the case during the weekend. Marcus had even gone to the extent of asking his teachers for the assignments in advance. Even though he still watched music videos on occasion, he seemed to be much more disciplined. At this academic pace, the week flew by in no time. By Friday, the Wright brothers thought that they would begin the tough job of reviewing some of the items in the circus store.

"There are a lot of items on that list," said Havier.

"Yeah," replied Marcus.

"We'd better head to the circus supply store right away," Havier commented.

"Ok," said Marcus confidently.

The young detectives left the house that Friday afternoon and headed for the subway station. They did not speak at all on the train ride. Instead, they spent the time reading over the list of items that were purchased by the Black circus. The Wright brothers had made an extra copy of the list so that each of them could have one.

"Yo Havier, check this out," said Marcus holding a section of the list which read: 'Specially Ordered Items.' "I see someone ordered throwing knives."

"Knives? I don't remember any knife act in the circus, do you?" asked Havier.

"No. I think we're onto something," said Marcus.

"We'll check it out when we get to the circus supply store."

"Aight."

A few minutes passed by and Marcus noticed something else, "What about this ski mask. Do you think it was used in the crime?"

"It could have been," Havier responded.

There were so many specially ordered items that could have been clues or used in the crime such as a baseball bat, a pair of handcuffs and a straight jacket. Then there were other specially ordered items that couldn't even be used in a circus.

"Why would someone need a car cover?" asked Marcus.

"And check this out: 'three fishing poles.' There are no fishing poles used in the circus," Havier said to his younger brother.

"This is a strange section of the list."

"We'll have to ask Mr. Brunson about these items."

"But they're so many. I mean, an MP3 player? What does a person in a circus need an MP3 player for?"

"I guess we'll just have to find out."

The remainder of the ride was short and without conversation.

"Hi Mr. Brunson," Havier greeted the inventory manager as they approached his fourth floor counter.

"You two detectives decided to return for some sleuthing?" Mr. Brunson asked.

"Yes, sir," replied Havier politely.

"Well, how can I help you?"

"There are so many items to look at on the list that we're not sure where to start," said Marcus.

"Well even though you began looking at the items last week, why don't you start at the top of the list and work downward. It's probably important that you see every item on the list. That would be my advice. Don't miss anything at all. Unless, of course, you have a direct clue about Zauditu's disappearance that would make you want to look at a particular item or group of items. If that's the case then I would narrow my search to those items that are important."

"Actually, we have many clues, but we haven't figured out what they mean," said Havier.

"So you don't know where to start. Well, like I said, start at the top of the list and work down," said Mr. Brunson.

"We were thinking that, because it was a kidnapping, some restraint items or weapons might have been used," explained Havier.

"You two seem hot on the trail of the suspect."

"Yes, we are. We thought that the items listed as: 'Special Ordered Items' might help us. We noticed that a few of them are restraint items and items that could be used as weapons," said Havier.

"Listen," Mr. Brunson said while leaning over the counter and lowering his voice, "the circus folks order a lot of things. I mean strange things that I never saw in a circus before. But most of the performers are honest. The circus management gets the list and they approve each and every item by initialing next to it. I think it's their way of saying 'thank you' to the circus performers. Most of the time, the circus performers use the items for some sort of new act. For example, that MP3 player was used by one of the clowns to learn his dancing routine. Usually, I just order the items because I know that the majority of the circus performers are honest."

"Do you mind if we look at some of the specially ordered items?" asked Marcus.

"Sure, but you know that many of the specially ordered items aren't here. Some of them were just ordered, so they did not arrive yet. And if they arrived, they may have been picked up from the store already. If they are here, they would be over there," Mr. Brunson pointed to a shelf in the corner of the store.

"Thanks, we'll get to work," said Marcus.

"Good luck," said Mr. Brunson.

A review of the specially ordered items shelf showed that many of the items had not arrived, or had already been picked up. However, some were there. Of particular interest was a set of throwing knives. Marcus spotted them first.

"Havier, these are the knives that were on the list!" Marcus said pointing to the knives.

Havier rushed over to the box that held the knives and examined them.

"This box is brand new," he observed.

"Yeah, if we could open it that would be great," replied Marcus.

"Let's ask."

"Ok."

"Mr. Brunson, we found an item that we would like to see. It's brand new in the plastic," said Havier.

Mr. Brunson examined the box of throwing knives that Havier was holding and said, "I can't open an item like that; one that's brand new in the plastic. That set arrived yesterday. Two sets were specially ordered by the Black circus two weeks before they arrived to perform in New York. One of them got here before the circus had its first show, the other set just got here. I'm probably going to have to return it because the person who ordered it doesn't want the knives anymore. In fact, you can take a look at this other set of throwing knives that was recently returned. Come behind the counter and I will show them to you."

The two young detectives walked around and followed Mr. Brunson into a small room behind the counter.

"You said that the knives were recently returned, who was it who ordered the knives?" Marcus asked.

"Ralph the Magnificent Magician ordered them and then returned the set. He bought them right before the Black circus had its first show. He returned them on Thursday of this week. He said he didn't need them anymore and that their purpose had been served. He also said that those things were lethal and could kill."

"Wow, did he use those exact words? I mean 'lethal and could kill'?" Havier asked excitedly.

"Yep," Mr. Brunson responded dispassionately.

"I don't trust this whole situation. Could we take a closer look at the knives he returned?" Havier inquired with suspicion.

"Sure, right this way," said Mr. Brunson while taking them to an old box that was sitting on the shelf. "This is the box that Ralph the magician returned the knives in. Feel free to look through it as much as you want.

The knives were scattered haphazardly throughout the cardboard box.

Havier read the sign that had been stamped on the side of the box. "Return to company."

"Most of these knives look brand new," said Marcus.

"Yeah."

"Some of them are hard to see because they are under the others. I think we better use a stick or something to move the knives on top. That way if we need them for evidence, we won't have messed them up with our fingerprints."

"Good idea Marcus," Havier said while reaching for one of those grabbers that is used to take items off of the top shelf.

The Wright brothers moved the knives one at a time.

"These don't look like they were even used," Marcus noted.

Then, at the bottom of the pile of knives, a few knives of interest emerged. There were three knives in all.

"Check out that one. It has nicks all up and down it," Havier observed.

"And the other two look like they have some reddish-brown stuff on them."

"That's not reddish-brown stuff Marcus. That looks like dried blood!"

"Dried blood?" shouted Marcus.

"Yeah, that's what I said, dried blood. And that means if it is dried blood that whoever had this knife might have hurt Zauditu."

"Ralph the Magnificent Magician had it. I bet he was the one that hurt Zauditu. He did it!" Marcus hastily concluded.

"Let's not jump to stupid conclusions. Yeah, it looks like it was him, but it could be someone else," said Havier in a measured tone.

"Someone else? There's blood on those knives and what did Ralph the magician say when he came in here? He said that the knives were lethal and could kill, and he also said that they served their purpose. When you put that with the fact that only three of the knives look like they'd been used, he's guilty. Look, if he had got the knives to use in some knife throwing act, then they would all be dented up or none of them would have dents. He would've used all of them to practice. Plus, two of them wouldn't have blood on them," Marcus sounded like an attorney in a court room.

"Well, Ralph's clue led to Mr. Collins…" Havier began to reply, but Marcus wasn't done.

"Forget about that. Ralph probably used the knives, one in each hand, to commit the crime. He used them as deadly weapons. And remember the way he was acting when we went to see him. All that disappearing and laughing when he reappeared. It all fits together and makes sense. That's the laugh of a guilty man," Marcus concluded his argument.

Havier was amazed that his younger brother was able to put together most of the clues into such a convincing argument.

He praised his younger brother, "I have to admit that you're probably right Marcus. I think we should turn these knives over to Captain James. I'm sure he could figure out if Ralph the Magnificent Magician did it."

At that moment Mr. Brunson came in the back to see how the Wright brothers were doing.

As he entered the back room where the Wright brothers were standing, Havier said, "Mr. Brunson we identified a substance on some of the knives. They might have been used in Zauditu's disappearance. Do you mind if we take the knives to Captain James in the police department?"

"Sure, if you think that they have something to do with Zauditu's disappearance then you can take them. Please make sure that you bring the box of knives directly to Captain James because I have to mark the item under a special category on my inventory list. I never had to do this before, but there is a company provision for items under investigation by law enforcement officials. I'm going to check with the police department this evening to make sure that they received the box of knives. If not, I'll have to call your parents," Mr. Brunson said firmly.

"We understand, Mr. Brunson. We want to help solve the case and we will bring the box of knives right to the precinct," said Marcus.

"When you turn it in they will assign an evidence number for the Zauditu case. You be sure to get that number. Call me here as soon as you get it," Mr. Brunson said, handing the Wright brothers a card containing the phone number to the circus store.

"Ok, Mr. Brunson," said Havier and the two young detectives left the shop with the box that had been carefully placed into several plastic garbage bags to protect the evidence.

"Mr. Brunson was acting kind of strange toward the end of our time at the circus store," said Marcus.

"Well, he was nervous about trusting us with the knives. He was nice enough to give us the knives. He didn't have to do that. I think he just wanted to cover his inventory and job."

"True that," Marcus agreed.

The two young men took the box directly to the precinct, but did not expect Captain James to be there.

"Is Captain James here?" Havier asked one of the two African-American police officers who were sitting at the front desk. "I'm Havier Wright and this is my brother Marcus."

"Captain James mentioned you two. You don't have to say anymore young brothers. I'll get him right away," said the officer.

"Wow, he's working on a Friday night?" inquired Marcus.

"Captain James has a big job to do. Some weeks he works every day," the officer explained.

"I see," said Marcus.

Within two minutes Captain James had emerged from the rear of the precinct.

"Hi, Captain James," said Havier.

"How are my two detectives doing?" Captain James asked with a smile.

"We found some possible evidence in the disappearing acrobat case," Havier stated.

"What did you find?"

"Ralph the Magnificent Magician had specially ordered these knives from *Party Hardy Now and Circus Enterprises*. It's a store in downtown Manhattan," said Havier.

"Mr. Brunson is one of the managers there. He allowed us to take the knives as long as we turned them in to you. He wanted us to call him when we got a chance and to give him the evidence number for Zauditu's case so that he knows that we officially registered the knives as evidence. He should be at the store for a few more hours this evening," said Marcus.

"What's the number? I'll call him right now."

Havier handed Captain James the card containing the number and he made the call.

"Thanks, fellows," said Captain James hanging up. "You two are turning into mighty fine detectives. I'm going to have to add you to my squad in a few years."

"Thanks," said Marcus.

"Our conversation about the knives was halted because I had to make that phone call. Was there something special about them that I should know?" Captain James inquired.

"Yes, one of the knives had been nicked up pretty bad. Two of the other knives have some dried substance on them that looks like dried blood," said Marcus.

"Really, did you guys touch the knives?"

"No sir. We used one of those grabber things to reach items on the top shelf of the store to move the knives one-by-one. That's when we noticed the three knives in question," explained Havier.

"Then there's a good chance that any fingerprints that were on the knives are still there. I'll turn the knives over to the officers in the Bronx who are assigned to the case. They'll check for DNA evidence and for fingerprints. The officers in the Bronx have several of Zauditu's personal items in an evidence room. I'm sure that they'll be able to crosscheck the DNA on these knives with Zauditu's DNA. The only problem is that testing for DNA can take several weeks," said Captain James.

"And the Black circus will only be here for three more weeks," said Marcus.

"Exactly, there are only three weekend performances after this weekend. However, I'm sure the detectives in the Bronx know that they have to put a rush on the testing process in order to get it done on time."

"Is there anything else we can do?" asked Havier.

"Just keep being the great detectives that you are and feel free to come see me anytime," said Captain James in a reassuring tone.

The Wright brothers left the precinct. It was getting late so they headed home. The next day, Saturday, would be a long day of sleuthing.

Chapter 11: Back to the Circus

The next logical place for the Wright brothers to go was back to the circus. If they were careful, then they might be able to find out some more information about Ralph the Magnificent Magician and his suspected role in the disappearance of Zauditu. Even though the budding detectives could have used their media passes to watch the circus again, they were more focused upon questioning Ralph. They arrived after the early show on Saturday.

"We'll have plenty of time to question Ralph," said Marcus.

"Yeah," Havier responded.

The Wright brothers showed their media passes and then entered the circus.

"Let's go check Ralph's tent," said Havier.

Marcus popped his head through the entrance to Ralph's tent and exclaimed with disappointment, "He's not here!"

"Relax Marcus, he probably just stepped out the tent or something."

The Wright brothers waited for about fifteen minutes.

"I'm tired of this. I don't want to wait anymore," said Marcus impatiently.

"Let's just wait five or ten minutes longer," Havier pushed.

"Aight."

After a few minutes, Eric the clown passed by. He seemed to be in a hurry.

"Hi Eric, do you know where Ralph the Magnificent Magician went?" asked Havier.

"Probably lunch," he said in a nervous tone.

"Thanks," replied Havier.

The Wright brothers decided to wait until Ralph returned. Even if it meant a long wait, it would be worthwhile to see him.

One hour slowly elapsed and Marcus said impatiently, "Havier let's be out. This cat isn't coming."

"Let's wait a few more minutes. He might be late from lunch."

Another twenty minutes elapsed, but there was no sign of Ralph. However, Kia walked by and said hello to the two detectives.

"Hi Kia," said Marcus.

"Hi," she responded in a gentle tone.

"Do you know when Ralph is going to get back from lunch?" inquired Marcus.

"Lunch? I haven't seen Ralph all day long. I don't think he came in today," said Kia.

"Why wouldn't he come in? Isn't he part of the circus?" asked Havier.

"Well, as you probably know, his act has been put on hold until Zauditu is found. So he's really here to morally support the rest of us. The only problem is well…" Kia stopped abruptly.

"What were you going to say?" Havier inquired.

"Yeah, what were you going to say?" Marcus pushed.

"It's just that Ralph is very antsy without much to do in the show. You know he is always trying to introduce some new act or some new magic trick into the show. It must be very hard on him. He's just here with nothing to do," said Kia.

"Do you know what was the most recent act he wanted to introduce into the show?" asked Havier.

"Yeah, it was a knife throwing act. After about a week, he gave it up."

"Is there anything else that you can tell us about Ralph?" asked Havier.

Kia hesitated, "Uh…well he loves donuts and he often hangs out with Eric the clown and Jake the animal trainer. They're always talking about how they have to handle their business. When they know very well that the only real business that they have is working for the circus."

"Eric seems to be very level headed. But what about Jake the animal trainer?" asked Havier.

"Eric is one of the nicest people in the Black circus. He would never harm a fly. But Jake the animal trainer, he's a different story. Why he does all kinds of crazy things to those animals to get them to do what they do in the circus," said Kia.

"What do you mean?" inquired Marcus.

"You know don't you? All those things animal trainers do to the animals. They do all kinds of mean things. Sometimes I think he has no heart."

"Really?" Marcus inquired.

"Yes, and the way that he acts," she paused momentarily, "he's a shady character."

"What do you mean?" asked Marcus with interest in his voice.

"He's always running around as though he's in a hurry. You can be in the middle of a conversation with him and he'll announce that he has to go. Then he'll just run out of the room. He's been that way for years. But lately, he's also been acting extra agitated," said Kia.

"In what way?" asked Havier.

"He's been very angry. The other day I asked him how he was doing and he yelled at me. Then I asked him why he was so mad. He said that it's too bad that Zauditu went so easily. He said that he could have single handedly saved her if he had intervened sooner. I asked him what he meant, but he just mumbled something and said never mind. He seemed deeply disturbed. I think that he was very bothered about Zauditu's disappearance."

"Do you know where Jake the animal trainer was when Zauditu disappeared?" asked Havier.

"Yeah, he was backstage in a tent getting the animals ready for entrance onto the circus floor. That's his job. He has to train the animals, get them ready and manage them during the show. When the circus is running, he has a lot of work to do all by himself."

"So he doesn't have any help?" Marcus queried Kia.

"Well for most of the show he has no help at all. Sometimes he gets a little help from Eric and Mary. I must say though, he does an amazing job getting all those animals together and ready for us. Maybe that's why he's so agitated all of the time. Sometimes he and Ralph work together to make a tiger or elephant appear in the middle of the circus arena. Don't ask me how they do it, but it must take some pretty amazing coordination between the two of them," said Kia.

"Is Jake in his tent right now?" asked Havier.

"No, I think he and Eric said that they were going to be in their favorite spot in Central Park today," added Kia.

"Did they say what they were going to be doing?" Havier inquired.

"No, but I assume they are going to 'handle their business' if you know what I mean. Those guys are just too much. All talk and no action. I assume they're just enjoying themselves in the park," she said while laughing.

"Central Park is a big place Kia. We wanted to ask them a few questions if we could. Do you have any idea where they would be?" asked Havier.

"Absolutely, they would be in the same place they always are when the circus comes to town. In fact, it's really not just their spot in the park. Many of us: Eric, Jake, Mary, Ralph and even myself and some of the other clowns and acrobats hang out there. There's a nice little pond there you would really like," said Kia writing down directions to the place in the park.

"Do they ever go elsewhere in Central Park?" asked Marcus.

"Yes, but rarely. Here are the directions to the area. It's actually quite secluded in that section of the park. You get a few people passing by, but for the most part, the area is tranquil."

"Thanks Kia, you have really helped us out a lot today," said Havier.

"I just hope that Zauditu is found as quickly as possible," Kia said with a sigh.

"So do we," Marcus added.

The detectives headed quickly to the circus exit because they felt an urgency to get to the park.

Chapter 12: A Conversation in the Park

The Wright brothers exited the subway and walked a few blocks over to Central Park. The initial area that they entered was filled with an assortment of park visitors. Foreigners walked beside the city's residents. Bike riders and rollerbladers sped through the park's concrete paths. Young children seemed to enjoy the break from the harsh city life.

The Wright brothers made their way down the park path. Kia's directions quickly led them away from the crowds and to a side path. One or two people occasionally walked by the young men as they headed toward their destination. After a few minutes of walking through the woods, the two detectives emerged in a clearing. A small pond reflected the rays of the sun.

"There they are," whispered Marcus who had spotted Eric and Jake.

The two men were walking toward the woods on the other side of the pond.

"Hold up Marcus. Let's wait and watch for a minute," said Havier.

Eric and Jake walked off the path and disappeared into the woods.

"Come on let's go Havier!"

"I think we should be more cautious."

"We can't wait and watch anymore because there's nothing to watch!" Marcus pressured his older brother.

"Ok let's go," Havier conceded.

The Wright brothers walked quickly around the pond to the spot where the two circus performers had disappeared.

"You think we should go after them?" Havier asked with some hesitation.

"Isn't that why we came over here?"

"Well I guess we could try to follow them so that they don't notice us."

"I'm feeling that," responded Marcus.

The two sleuths entered the wooded area with caution. The forest floor was covered with matted leaves from several years of buildup. Havier and Marcus carefully made their way into the woods. After a short time, they came to a small clearing and heard Eric's and Jake's voices. Havier and Marcus could see a small stream running below them. The landscape dropped off sharply about ten feet down. Thus, the Wrights were essentially looking down upon the circus employees. Eric the clown and Jake the animal trainer were seated on a rock on the other side of the stream. Fortunately, there were several large boulders in the area. Havier and Marcus quickly crouched behind a large boulder and listened.

"It's all elementary to me. After being stabbed, she's gone forever. And if that wasn't enough, he stabbed her again. An aspiring acrobat like that, gone forever," said Jake.

"Yeah, but you know that you had a role in that entire affair. You were the one who tied her down," Eric emphasized.

"Yeah, but you were the one who convinced her to come with us in the first place. You're just as guilty as me. He stabbed her right in front of our eyes, and you didn't stop him. You let him do it again. It was your big mouth that got us into this situation. Without your mouth we wouldn't be in this mess Eric."

"And now she's gone."

"I just want this whole thing to go away, but I know it won't. Then you've got those two Wright kids snooping around about Zauditu's disappearance. I'm really afraid that they might find out something that they shouldn't know," Jake said in a worried tone.

"I know what you mean Jake, but just stay cool, calm and collected when they come around. They're only kids and they don't know what they're doing."

Jake was agitated, "Cool, calm and collected? I can't be cool, calm and collected. Do you know how bad it would look if the public found out all of the facts? Forget about a circus suspension, they would parade us in front of the media."

"Yeah, but if the Wright brothers come around asking questions and you remain calm then no one will ever find out what happened."

"Those two fellows are really sneaky. I think they might find out something that they're not supposed to know. In fact, I think they know too much already. And you Eric, you're always running off at the mouth; telling them this or that about the circus. You're liable to slip up and mention something about the incident."

"Ok, but you know that if Zauditu is never found, the circus won't go on. I might be able to help them find her once and for all, if you know what I mean. You and I both know she's not alive. So, if the Wright brothers find her body they would be heroes, the circus management would bring closure to the case, the circus would go on, and our jobs would be intact," Eric argued.

"Anything you say will incriminate you. The very fact that you give them information to find Zauditu dead as a doornail would get you locked up," the animal trainer added.

"Yeah, well I think I can remedy all of this mess. The police don't know about the incident and I don't think that two teenagers are going to be able to find out anything from me. The way I see it is the more I can divert their attention, the better. I believe the Wright brothers think highly of me and they will listen to what I say."

"So what if they start asking questions about the knives or stabbing. What are you going to tell them? Are you going to lie to them?"

"Don't worry about it Jake. I'll handle them. You just focus on handling those animals. That's a big job you've got there and we can't afford for you to get all stressed and mess it up."

"Well, I'm going to avoid those two Wright brothers at all costs. I will answer no questions at all. And if they approach me, I'm out. You can't learn what you can't see or talk to. Those Wright brothers are trouble I tell you. Trouble!"

"And what are you going to say if the police come and start asking questions? You can't just disappear then. You have to deal with them on some level at least."

"Well, the police are different. I'll give them vague answers if they come around. But they'll get no clues from me, Eric."

"Ok, I'll also deal with the cops if they come around. I just don't want to have this whole thing exposed and I'm going to use my gift of gab to cover it up," Eric enunciated with confidence.

"Well, no one's getting a word out of me. No one!" Jake said firmly while giving an African handshake to Eric.

Marcus was tired of squatting behind the large rock. He decided to realign his feet by shifting them slightly. In the process he stepped on a small twig and it made a snapping noise. Normally, this sound wouldn't have been out of the ordinary, but the two circus employees were on edge because of the nature of their conversation.

"I think someone's coming Eric," Jake warned.

"Let's be out," said Jake in a soft voice.

"We can dip out the other side of the woods."

The two men began to head in the opposite direction of the Wright brothers.

"We can split up when we exit the woods," the animal trainer whispered loudly.

Havier and Marcus allowed the men to move quite a distance away before they made even the slightest move.

"Let's follow them!" Marcus whispered in an excited tone.

"No, it's too dangerous," said Havier.

"We already came this far. We might as well follow them."

"This is going to get us into big problems."

"Come on, Hav!" Marcus pushed.

"Ok, give them more of a lead and then we'll follow them," Havier conceded.

The Wright brothers followed the men. Even though the men were a good distance ahead of them, Havier and Marcus were very cautious. They hid behind trees and rocks as they followed Eric and Jake. After a few minutes of this pursuit, the men exited the woods.

"Looks like they're splitting up," said Havier.

"Who do you think we should follow?" asked Marcus.

"We'll I don't think we should split up. Either one of them could overpower us in a one-on-one situation," Havier wisely thought out loud.

"I think we should follow Jake."

"I hear that."

Chapter 13: Following the Animal Trainer

The Wright brothers hid cautiously in the woods. On the other side was an empty path. They watched as Eric walked towards the left and then disappeared out of sight. They also watched Jake as he walked to the right.

From their hiding spot in the woods Marcus said, "Come on Havier he's almost out of sight."

"Ok let's follow him," Havier replied cautiously.

The Wright brothers shadowed Jake until the walkway opened into one of the main park paths. Jake entered the crowd of park strollers, bike riders and rollerbladers. The two detectives blended into the throng and kept an eye on Jake who was about one block ahead of them. He exited the park and began to walk down one of the city's side streets.

"Make sure he doesn't dip," said Marcus.

"Aight, I'm watching him," replied Havier.

The Wright brothers turned the corner and spotted Jake toward the middle of the next block. This methodical pursuit kept on going for a few blocks.

"Look, he went into that store," Marcus pointed out.

"Yeah I see."

"You think we should go into the store?"

"Nah, let's hang back for a minute."

The store was a small delicatessen with a yellow awning and red lettering.

"He's taking a long time," Marcus said impatiently.

"He'll be out soon," said Havier.

"You think he saw us following him and dipped?" asked Marcus.

"No, where would he go?"

"Out the back of the deli. A lot of these stores got a back exit."

"And where is he going then? Usually the back exits lead to some alleyway or something that's blocked off," Havier explained.

"This is Jake the snake we're talking about here. When we chased him from the barber shop, he was ghost. We couldn't stop him and neither could a barbed wire fence," Marcus commented.

"You ever thought about how he was able to do that?" Havier inquired.

"Probably from training all those animals."

"True that. That's tough work. He probably got to climb up on elephants and all that," Havier added.

At that moment Jake exited the store carrying a small paper bag and a soda.

"You think he's having a late lunch or an early dinner?" asked Marcus.

"I don't know, but we should keep following him."

Jake continued walking the length of Manhattan's streets. He turned down one street and then down another.

"Where is this cat going?" asked Havier.

"I don't know. Hope he ain't trying to dip us."

"Please, if Jake wanted to be out he would. He didn't see us yet," Havier responded with confidence.

After about one half hour of walking Jake entered a large store which sold circus and party supplies. It was not the same store that Mr. Brunson worked at.

"Should we follow him?" asked Marcus.

"It looks like a lot of people are in there. Look how many people are coming and going from the store. He'll never see us if we blend in with the crowds. Let's follow him."

The Wright brothers entered the store and paused at the entrance.

"Look, there he goes," Marcus pointed through the crowd of shoppers to a counter at the right of the store.

"He's talking to that man. It looks like the man is asking him something," said Havier.

"Look the man is nodding his head. Now he's telling Jake something."

Jake walked toward the Wright brothers.

"Here he comes, let's be out," said Marcus.

The Wright brothers exited the circus store quickly, crossed the street and entered a store where they watched for Jake. By the time Jake left the store, the two detectives had blended into the scene of streetwalkers.

"Let's follow him some more," said Marcus with enthusiasm.

"The Wright brothers tailed Jake for a few blocks. Jake disappeared behind the sign of a subway entrance. Havier and Marcus darted toward the stairs of the subway entrance.

"There he is," Marcus said after catching a glimpse of Jake near the bottom of the stairs.

"Let's follow him!" replied Havier entering the stairway.

"Faster, we're going to loose him!" said Marcus as they descended the stairs.

The subway station below was very large. Several hundred people were coming and going to and from the trains.

"Do you see him?" asked Havier.

"No. How about you?" Marcus queried his older brother.

The Wright brothers decided to walk through the station looking for Jake. After about ten minutes of no luck Marcus said, "Do you think he'll show up."

"No. We lost him in the crowd."

"So what should we do now?"

"Let's go back to that store and speak to the man Jake was talking to," said Havier.

"Aight, sounds good to me."

The Wright brothers headed back to the circus and party supply store.

"There he is, right at that counter," Marcus said pointing out the obvious.

The two detectives approached the tall slender Caucasian man.

"Hello sir, my name is Havier and we were trying to find out some information about Jake the animal trainer from the Black circus for a media story we're working on," Havier said throwing up his media pass.

"I don't know Jake that well, but what information were you looking for?" the man asked cautiously.

"Well, what does he normally buy from you?" asked Marcus.

"He has come in here a few of times with that clown Eric. Usually they just order stuff for the circus," said the man.

"What kind of stuff?" asked Marcus.

"Well, as you know Jake is an animal trainer. He uses all types of sticks and prods to train them. And Eric is a clown so he orders clown costumes and other clown things," the tall man explained.

"Prods?" asked Marcus.

"Yeah you know those sticks with semi-sharpened metal on the end that they use to poke elephants and horses with when they don't listen?"

"Could you hurt someone with those things?" asked Marcus.

"If you can hurt an Elephant with a prod, then you could easily hurt a man," said the tall skinny man.

"Are there any other items that Jake or Eric has bought?" Havier inquired.

"Not really, mostly stuff like gloves and harnesses to handle the animals."

"What about any other weapons like knives or guns?" Marcus pushed the issue.

"Not really. Before they came to town, he called the store and said he was going to order some knives for his friend the magician. Then he told me that he didn't need them anymore. When he got here, he said that his friend the magician was able to get them pretty quickly from the circus' normal supplier," said the tall man.

"What's your impression of Eric and Jake?" asked Havier.

The tall man answered Havier's question, "You mean his character? "Well, Jake and Eric are both nice guys. Jake is kind of quiet, you know. On the other hand, Eric likes to talk a lot more."

"Would it be possible if we could see your inventory? I mean only the items that Jake the animal trainer ordered from you?" Marcus pushed further.

"Sorry, I don't think that would be possible. Why would you need an inventory list for a news story on the circus?" asked the tall man.

"Well we're also trying to find out some information about the disappearance of the acrobat from the circus," Marcus blurted out.

"Oh, I see. Do you think Jake and Eric had a role in her disappearance?" asked the tall manager.

"Right now we're just trying to get some more information about her disappearance," Havier interjected.

"Well I really don't have anymore information for you guys."

"Thanks for everything, sir," said Haiver.

"Yeah, thanks," Marcus added.

The Wright brothers exited the store and walked while discussing their next move.

Chapter 14: A Test of the Equipment

The mystery of the disappearing acrobat was only thickening. The Wright brothers felt that they had gathered a tremendous amount of evidence against several of the circus employees. However, a number of key mysteries had to be uncovered. The two things that perplexed them most pertained directly to the way that Zauditu disappeared and her present whereabouts.

"Where do you think Zauditu is?" asked Marcus.

"I'm not sure," replied Havier.

"It sounds like they took her out."

"If they did how come she didn't turn up in some alleyway or something?" Havier queried his younger brother.

"I'm not so sure about that. You heard Eric and Jake talking in the park. They probably just hid the body."

"You know what's really bothering me?"

"What?"

"How did Zauditu disappear? I mean I was watching and you were watching," Havier stated.

"Yeah, there were thousands of people watching and not one of them saw who took Zauditu. That just don't make sense," Marcus agreed with his older brother.

"Yeah it doesn't make sense at all."

"Do you think we could find out how she disappeared?" asked Marcus.

"What do you mean?" Marcus' older brother asked.

"I mean if we checked out the circus equipment we might find out how Zauditu disappeared or some other clue about the case."

"Yeah, yeah, I like that idea. Word."

The Wright brothers headed over to the circus that Saturday evening. They figured that they could test the equipment after the late show. They arrived at the circus just as the show had ended and waited until almost all of the performers had left. Using their media passes, they entered the arena. It was about 9:30pm when they arrived.

Havier and Marcus walked among the circus equipment. There were large drum-like objects that the elephants rested their feet on. Havier carefully inspected one of them to see if it would yield a clue. However, he found nothing out of the ordinary.

There was also a semicircle that bordered the front of the circus arena. It was about two feet high. Ralph the magician often stood outside of this circle when he did his magic tricks. Marcus tapped the wood surrounding the circle.

"It looks solid to me," he said.

Two tall poles from which circus flags hung sat about twenty feet away from the semicircle wall. Havier inspected the poles but they yielded no clues.

Lastly, there were the trapezes and the trampolines. The four trampolines that were used by the acrobats were sitting under four of the trapezes. Marcus approached the trampoline and rested a hand on its edge.

"This trampoline is pretty high off of the ground," he observed.

"That's because they fly from the trapezes way up there," Havier said pointing up.

"This side looks the same as those other two trampolines," said Marcus who had walked around the trampoline.

"Yeah, looks the same to me too."

"Hey, Havier I thought the trampolines were a different color. The trampolines used in the circus we saw were white, and these are beige."

"Maybe they got dirty," said Havier.

"No those were different trampolines in the circus we saw."

"So, why do you think they got rid of those other trampolines?"

"There must be some trick with the other four trampolines," Marcus concluded.

The Wright brothers decided to look for the other trampolines. Few of the circus employees were left in the arena. On the outskirts of the arena were the tents. Ralph's tent, the tent for the animal trainer, several tents that were shared by the acrobats and clowns, an office tent for the management and some other unidentified tents surrounded the arena floor.

"Let's check Ralph's tent first. He probably didn't get back yet," said Marcus.

"Ok," responded Havier.

The Wright brothers announced themselves before entering the tent.

"This tent looks empty," Marcus commented.

"Except for that cabinet over there," Havier said pointing towards a tall cabinet on the left side of the tent that they had not formerly noticed.

"It has a big padlock on it."

"I wonder why we didn't notice it before."

"Because Ralph was doing all of those disappearing tricks. Plus he was giving us puns to solve. I'll tell you, he's not trustworthy. I bet he has some evidence he's hiding in there," said Marcus pointing to the cabinet.

"Probably, but remember his pun sent us to Mr. Collins. We must be balanced in our assessment of suspects."

"He's guilty and so is that animal trainer," Marcus concluded.

"I think so too, but we should let the police do their work with the fingerprinting and the DNA testing. In the meantime, let's keep looking for those trampolines."

The next tent that the Wright brothers decided to look in was Jake's tent. They announced their presence before they entered the tent, but it was also empty.

"Look there!" said Marcus pointing to a metal rod with a sharp hook-like object on the end of it.

"What's that?" Havier added.

The Wright brothers approached the hook, crouched down and examined it without touching it.

"Look, it has some dried reddish-brown stuff on its hook," said Marcus.

"Don't touch it," said Havier while pulling a bunch of cloth napkins and a garbage bag from his back pocket.

"What's that for?"

"That hook might be evidence. We shouldn't touch it with our hands. It might mess up any fingerprints that might be on it."

"Yeah, we should take it to Captain James."

Havier took the bag and carefully placed the hook in it.

"We'll have to turn that in to Captain James later tonight," Havier said with confidence.

"I don't see anything else important in this tent. Let's check another tent."

The Wright brothers began to look in tent after tent. As they had before, they were sure to announce their presence before entering any of the tents. For the most part, their examination of each tent was cursory. Looking for massive trampolines did not require much more than an eye scan of each tent. After examining many of the acrobats' and clowns' tents, the Wright brothers decided to look in a few of the unidentified tents. One of them contained the four white trampolines that, except for their beige color, looked like the other four on the circus floor. The four trampolines took up most of the tent floor space because they were placed side-by-side.

"Looks the same to me," said Marcus passing a hand over the edge of one of the trampolines.

"But look there. What's that?" Havier said looking at a slightly discolored patch to the left center of the surface of the trampoline.

"I'll climb up and check it out," Marcus said while climbing up on the trampoline. "Hav look, I'm flying dumb high!" Marcus exclaimed as he jumped on the trampoline.

"Stop clowning!" Havier said in an angry tone.

"Ok, ok I'll check out the spot."

"What is it?"

"It looks like a patch. Like the patches Mom and Dad used to put on their jeans back in the day. Except it's really covering the bottom of a hole. If you crawl under the trampoline, you could see what I'm talking about," Marcus explained.

The trampoline sat about five feet off of the ground. Havier crouched down, ducked his head and walked under the trampoline. When he got to the patch, he looked up and saw exactly what Marcus was talking about. It was a round circle of trampoline material, about three feet wide and it had a spring hinge. It contained a padded bar across its bottom and what appeared to be a release lever. Havier pulled the lever and the bar moved easily away from the patch.

"Press down on the patch," Havier instructed Marcus.

"Wow, that was easy!" Marcus exclaimed as the patch opened.

"A trapdoor!"

"That's how Ralph made the acrobats disappear in thin air. They must have jumped up in the air, were hidden by Ralph's smoke, landed on the trampoline and slid or bounced through the trapdoor!" Marcus said with enthusiasm.

"Normally they probably popped up after Ralph covered the hole with another cloud of smoke."

"Right, and when they wanted to disappear until the second half of the show, they just didn't come up through the trapdoor."

"That's brilliant!" said Havier.

"But how did they get off of the circus floor? Remember the trampolines had nothing around them. And they were at least seventy-five to one-hundred feet from one another. Do you think there was another trapdoor in the circus floor?" asked Marcus.

The Wright brothers darted to the center of the arena. A careful examination of the floor revealed no trapdoor.

"That's a puzzle, Marcus," said Havier.

"Yeah, how did they get out from under one trampoline and over to the other trampoline? And when they finally disappeared, how did they get off of the floor? They couldn't have come out during intermission because some people who stayed in their seat would've seen them," Marcus thought out loud.

"Think back. Did they have any chance to escape?" asked Havier.

"I don't remember any."

"Wait! What about Jake?"

"What about him?" Marcus responded with an inquisitive tone.

As he walked over to the exact spot where one of the trapdoor trampolines was located, Havier began to gesture while thinking out loud, "Jake releases all kinds of animals onto the floor. The biggest one of these is the elephant. I bet the acrobats hid behind an elephant to move from trampoline to trampoline, and to exit the circus floor during intermission."

"That's a good thought Havier. However, the performance is watched from all angles in the arena. That means that someone must've seen the acrobats walking behind the elephants, and they would've told the police. Captain James would've told us. If you were hiding behind an elephant and walking, half the audience in the arena would see you and half the audience wouldn't," Marcus argued.

"True that," Havier replied with disappointment in his voice.

"I think the elephant idea was good. Do you have any more ideas about how they got the acrobats off the circus arena floor?"

"I still think it has something to do with those elephants. Only circus animals and the clowns that rode them were near the trampolines."

At that moment the Wright brothers saw Kia approaching them as they stood in the center of the arena.

"Hi, Kia," said Havier.

"Hi, fellows. I just came back to get something I left in my tent."

"We were wondering something Kia. It is something about the trap doors in the trampolines. We know that Ralph the magician makes puffs of smoke appear so that the acrobats can slide through the trap doors unnoticed. We think that the acrobats use the elephants to exit from the main circus arena floor. We just can't figure out how," Havier enumerated.

"Well, I see you two have discovered Ralph's masterful trick. I suppose that explaining the rest won't spoil the show much more," said Kia.

"Thanks, Kia," Marcus interjected.

"No problem. The way Ralph gets the acrobats from one trampoline to another and off of the floor is by using the elephants. If you noticed, all of the elephants have a harness on them that holds a place for the clowns to ride on top of them. Well, the harness also contains a box that is attached to the elephant's stomachs. The boxes hold up to three skinny people. Since acrobats are in shape, we fit three acrobats in the boxes."

Kia continued, "The way that the acrobats get in is by basically climbing in the box and then scooting all the way in so that another acrobat can enter. All of this is done when the elephants stop in front of the trampolines. As you can imagine, this trick takes a tremendous amount of coordination."

"But can't people see the acrobats climb into the boxes under the elephants?" asked Marcus.

"Yes and no," Kia replied.

"What do you mean?" Marcus followed up on his inquiry.

"Because people sit all around the arena, a select few of them can see the acrobats climbing into the boxes under the elephants. However, unless they are trained magicians, they would probably miss seeing the acrobats. This is because the acrobats do not climb under the elephants, unless Ralph has made one of those puffs of smoke in the air. Of course the booming sound of the smoke puffs distracts the audience enough so that the acrobats can enter the boxes under the elephants. It's all based on the art of distraction."

"You know that I watched a famous magician make an assistant appear in a box that was hanging at the top of the stage. The way that it was done was by having her climb up a ladder that was on top of an elephant. She did it in full view of the audience. However, there were so many other distracting events that were going on that the audience didn't even realize that she was setting up the magician's next trick. It's all about getting the audience to focus on one place while the magician is acting in another place," said Kia.

"Where do the acrobats go after they enter the boxes under the elephant?" asked Marcus.

"They wait until the elephant is led by one of the clowns to another trampoline with a trap door. The elephant walks around, then they scoot out of the box and roll under that trampoline. When the elephant walks away, Ralph creates a puff of smoke over the trap door. Each acrobat climbs through and does a little jump and flips as the smoke is clearing. This makes it seem as though the acrobat appeared out of thin air. Sometimes one acrobat leaves the elephant and sometimes two or three of them leave the elephant. In other words, three acrobats could be on one trampoline and then be made to appear on another trampoline," Kia explained.

"So that's how they do it? The elephant walks around and the acrobats climb in and then climb out. I guess that's what Ralph meant by 'a blast a saunter.' It was the elephants that were sauntering not Ralph when he disappeared in the tent," Marcus said turning to Havier.

"Yes, unless it's right before the intermission. Then the acrobats are brought to Jake the animal trainer's tent. Sometimes they are brought in one at a time. Sometimes they come in groups of two or three. It depends on how many acrobats are located under a trampoline. After the acrobats climb out of the boxes, the elephants are carefully lined up in order, and then they are walked back out on the floor to pick up more acrobats." said Kia.

"So I guess Jake was there when Zauditu arrived?" Marcus inquired.

"Actually he wasn't. Eric and Mary were in Jake's tent when Zauditu was supposed to arrive. Like I told you before, sometimes they help out Jake because he's overworked. In fact, Mary does not participate in Ralph's disappearing acrobat trick. She is the only one who is not included. Instead, Mary and Eric sometimes walk into Jake's tent while the elephants containing acrobats are arriving.

"Now Zauditu was the last acrobat to be picked up by one of the elephants because her trampoline was furthest from the tent. When she didn't arrive, Eric and Mary were a little worried. But they thought she must have arrived during an earlier round of the elephants," Kia stated.

"Earlier round?" asked Havier.

"Yes, during the earlier rounds of the elephants, Jake was in his tent. He left when Eric and Mary arrived. Usually Zauditu is the last acrobat to exit the circus floor. When she didn't arrive, Eric and Mary assumed she had gotten there earlier. However, during the intermission, Jake said that Zauditu never arrived. She usually arrives last because of this acrobatic feat she does toward the end of the show, and she did it that day too."

"Really," Marcus showed interest in what Kia was saying.

"Yes, then the circus management was notified right away and the rest of the show was canceled."

"You mentioned that Jake wasn't in his tent with Eric and Mary. Do you know where he went?" asked Marcus.

"When he gets a break, he takes a few minutes away from the stress. He needs a break often before the intermission and takes one until the intermission is over. Eric and Mary usually tie up the final elephants and horses that are brought in by the clowns," said Kia.

"Do these horses help the acrobats disappear in any way?" asked Havier.

"No, the horses are used as a distraction. They just walk around, but don't serve any purpose for the magic trick. Of course they do a few of their own stunts, but that has nothing to do with making the acrobats disappear. As you saw in the show, Ralph stays on the floor making puffs of smoke until Zauditu makes her exit in the elephant. Then he returns to his tent."

"Alone?" asked Havier.

"Yes, he goes back by himself and takes a break. Then the ring announcer comes on and tells the audience about intermission," she said.

"Do you know where Ralph goes during the intermission?" Marcus asked.

"He usually just hangs out by himself. Sometimes he gets ready for the second half of the show and sometimes he goes off somewhere by himself."

"Thanks, Kia," said Marcus.

"Oh, and in case you were wondering, I was on the circus floor during the entire performance. I am the only clown who wears the outfit with a drum on the back. I usually pick up items during intermission. That day, I went to the management office during the intermission."

"You've been in the clear from the start. The managers told us you were there the first day we started investigating Zauditu's disappearance," Havier explained.

"Oh I see you two really do your homework. I just hope that you are able to find Zauditu. She is such a nice woman."

"Thanks again, Kia," Havier said waving as the Wright brothers headed toward the circus exit. They walked in silence because they were in deep thought about all of the information that they had uncovered that day.

They took the train home with the intent of bringing the hook-like pole to Captain James. Havier was careful with the object in the bag. The ride home was relatively quiet because the Wright brothers were thinking about their next move. When they got to the precinct, Marcus spoke first.

"Hello, sir," he said cordially to the Black officer sitting behind the desk at the precinct. "I'm Marcus Wright and this is my brother Havier. Could we please speak to Captain James?"

"One minute, please," the officer said politely while entering the rear of the precinct to get Captain James.

"Hi, Havier and Marcus. How have you guys been?" Captain James spoke with a welcoming voice as he came out of the door.

"Ok, Captain James. We have been making progress on the disappearance of the acrobat Zauditu," said Marcus proudly.

"That's great. What have you been able to uncover?"

Havier explained, "Well we think that Jake, the animal trainer may have had a role in the crime. There may be some other suspects too, but we're still trying to find more information or evidence to determine if they had a role in it.

"We found this pole with a hook on the end of it in Jake, the animal trainer's tent. It has a small amount of dried reddish-brown stuff on the end of it. We were very careful not to tamper with it when we put it in this bag. If there were any fingerprints on it, they should still be there."

"Yeah, we thought you might want to submit it for DNA and fingerprint testing," Marcus added.

"Thanks guys, I will turn it over to the detectives in the Bronx. I hope that they can get it done before the circus leaves town," said Captain James.

"Do you have any idea when the DNA test and fingerprint test on Ralph's knives will come back?"

"I believe it should be sometime this week. It's lucky that the police in the Bronx asked for several samples of Zauditu's DNA. They used some hair from a brush on her dressing table and some other samples obtained from her hotel room. Therefore, a match between Ralph's knives and her

DNA can be found. If Jake the animal trainer's hook has her DNA on it, we can also draw a match."

"Thanks again for everything. You two have really helped to move this case along," said Captain James complementing the Wright brothers.

"No, we have to thank you Captain James," said Havier.

The two sleuths went home feeling that they had accomplished much for the day. When they got home it was late and Mr. and Mrs. Wright were waiting up for their sons.

"How has all that sleuthing been working out?" Mr. Wright asked.

"Great Dad, we're on the case," replied Marcus.

"I hope it hasn't messed up your school studies," Mr. Wright said in a stern tone.

"Of course not Dad. In fact, Marcus is doing better than ever. He aced his last math exam and he does all of his homework in advance so that we can use the weekend to work on the case," Havier explained.

"When are your report cards going to be sent home?" asked Mrs. Wright.

"In three weeks," said Havier.

"Yeah in three weeks," Marcus added.

"I expect that they will reflect all of the hard school work you two have been doing," said Mr. Wright.

"That's right Havier and Marcus. We expect only good grades," said Mrs. Wright.

"They will be good Mom and Dad," Havier and Marcus said simultaneously as they headed to their room and went to sleep.

Chapter 15: A Magic Escape

It was Sunday morning, the Wright brothers had made several gains in the case, but they also had many questions that they wanted answered. They figured that Ralph the Magnificent Magician would be returning to the circus after his day off. Perhaps he could provide some information that would help the Wright brothers solve the case.

"Ralph should be there by the time the first show ends. Let's try to get to the circus about a half hour before it ends," Havier told Marcus.

"That means we should be out in about two hours," said Marcus.

The Wright brothers ate their breakfast, talked for a little while and headed to the circus. Upon their arrival, the circus was ending. The two detectives headed straight for the entrance to the tents. They waited for the attendees to file out of the arena and then they headed to Ralph's tent.

"Ralph are you in there?" Marcus said passing by the entrance to the tent.

Marcus and Havier heard Kia's voice behind them, "Ralph's not there. He didn't come in again today. I'm starting to get worried. I mean, we had one person disappear from this circus and we don't want another one to vanish."

"Why do you think something's wrong?" asked Marcus

"Ralph has never missed two days of work at the circus. I realize that his act has been suspended, so I'm not overly worried, but I'm still concerned. He's probably just depressed that he can't do his magic in front of crowds of people," Kia empathized.

"Do you know where Ralph might be?" Marcus asked.

"Well, I tried calling him this morning when I didn't see him. He didn't answer his phone. So I thought that he might be at our famous hangout spot in Central Park. I'm going to head over there in about a half hour. Do you guys want to come with me?"

"There are a few things that we want to check out here. I'm not sure how long that might take, but we'll probably be able to meet you there in a couple hours from now," Havier said.

"Sounds good to me. I hope to see you there," Kia said.

The Wright brothers spent the next hour looking for more information and evidence at the circus. If they could not question Ralph, they felt that Eric and Mary would be their next best option.

"Remember all of that nonsense Eric said in the park? We should question him," said Marcus.

The Wright brothers headed to Eric's tent. One of the clowns there told him that Eric had gone out to lunch and would return in about two hours. Then, they went to Mary's tent.

"Mary's not here," said one of the acrobats. "She left after the show. She said she didn't have breakfast and had to get something to eat."

The Wright brothers waited around for a few minutes. They were hoping Eric and Mary would return from lunch early. Eventually, they decided that getting in touch with Ralph was a priority. Eric and Mary would most likely be at the circus at a later point in time and they could be questioned then. The Wright brothers left for Central Park and talked on the way.

"I hope we get to speak to Ralph in the park," said Marcus.

"It's a long shot," Havier replied.

"I know. Finding someone anywhere in New York City can be difficult. Even when you think you know where they might be."

"Yeah, one time I tried to meet up with Damien and Eugene at the Thirty-Fourth Street subway station. Forget about it! That station is so big you'll never find someone unless you know exactly where to meet them."

"What are we going to ask him if we see him?"

That's a good question. Because we practically know everything that he could tell us," said Havier.

"Yeah, we know about the bloody knives, about the trampolines and the puffs of smoke. What else is there to know?"

"Well, we don't know where Zauditu is and we still don't have a motive. Why would someone kidnap her?" Havier observed.

"That's true," said Marcus.

The Wright brothers arrived in the park about two hours and fifteen minutes after they had spoken to Kia. When they got there Kia was seated on a bench facing the pond. It provided a vantage point from which one could see all who came and went from that section of the park.

"Were you waiting long, Kia?" asked Havier compassionately.

"No only a few minutes," she replied.

Have you seen Ralph by any chance?" asked Havier.

"No, not yet, but then again I just got here twenty minutes ago."

At that moment, the Wright brothers looked up and saw Mr. Billings strolling through the park. He approached them with a smile on his face.

"Hi, Havier and Marcus, what brings you to Manhattan today?" he asked.

"The case," replied Havier. "This is Kia, she's a clown in the Black circus."

"My name is Billings. It's nice to meet you Kia."

"Nice to meet you too," Kia responded.

"We were all hoping Ralph the Magnificent Magician shows up so we can ask him some questions. Kia thinks he might show up here," said Marcus.

"Ralph is stressed and he always comes here when he's stressed," Kia explained. "You might think that the Black Circus is a glamorous lifestyle, but it's not. They don't pay us too much and Ralph is a big spender. He wanted to buy an expensive magic trick. It cost fifty thousand dollars, but they don't pay us enough to buy that type of trick and the circus wouldn't buy it for him. It's like any entertainment industry—dancing, acting, singing, rapping—there's some fame involved and you get to see a lot of places, but there's not a whole lot of money in it."

Marcus seemed surprised, "Rappers? Most rappers are paid. They have chains, nice cars and million dollar contracts. Just check out the music videos and you'll see what I'm talking about."

"How many million dollar rappers do you know that have a million dollars for sure?" Mr. Billings interjected.

Marcus began to count them. "I don't know, maybe about fifteen or twenty," he said, stretching the actual number he knew.

"And how many young brothers want to become rappers? Millions right? That means that the odds of becoming a successful rapper are like one in several thousand and the odds of becoming a millionaire through rap are close to one in a million. It's sort of like the lottery, where they sell you a dream. If you were to save that dollar, it would go a lot further over the long run. But everyone wants fast money today, including rappers," said Mr. Billings.

Marcus felt he knew a lot more than Mr. Billings about the rap industry because he watched music television on a regular basis. Struggling, he questioned Mr. Billings, "But all the rappers in music videos have chains and expensive cars. And that's a lot more than fifteen or twenty. Almost every video has rappers with things that cost a lot of money."

"Those chains and fancy cars are owned by the record companies. They bring them in for the videos, put them on the rappers, and then take them off after they are done filming. Then we rhyme about being gangsters and thugs and we glorify that lifestyle. They're turning us into clowns and court jesters, and we don't even know it. If they keep clowning our people like this, all of our men will be kidnapped just like Zauditu—by the false hopes and deceitful maneuvers of a system designed to put them in jail—it's all a clown trick. *It's Just Like the Circus!*"

Kia added to what Mr. Billings was saying, "Entertainment is no easy life. It is a strenuous lifestyle that requires hard work and discipline. We spend many evenings preparing for hours before a show, and so do the most successful rappers. They don't just get a contract and then sit back. They spend many long days writing, working in the studio and on tour. Some of them work sixteen hour days. They work hard like you guys are working on this case," Kia explained.

Havier built upon what Kia was explaining, "Kia and Mr. Billings are right. Rappers, or rather MC's, are people who believe in the art of moving the crowd. Moving a live audience is what they focus upon and they realize that they are one aspect of hip-hop culture. Hip-hop is a culture that includes eight other elements: DJ's, break dancers, beat boxers, graffiti artists, street language, street knowledge, street fashion and street entrepreneurialism."

"That's right!" Kia exclaimed.

"Well, I'm going to be on my way," said Mr. Billings.

"Take care," said Havier.

"Be safe and good luck on the case," replied Mr. Billings as he walked away.

"Now Kia, what were you saying about Ralph and the trick?" asked Havier.

"Well Ralph really wanted this trick that used light and mirrors to make large objects like skyscrapers look like they disappeared. I mean, he really wanted it. He asked all of us to borrow some money. When we found out how much money it cost, we told him no because there was no way that he would be able to buy it. That's the first time I saw Ralph that angry. He stormed out of the circus that night and wouldn't speak to us for days. When we arrived in New York, he had just begun to speak to us again. He wanted money for the trick and he wanted it bad. He would have killed for that money if he could have," said Kia.

"Killed for it?" asked Marcus.

"Maybe I shouldn't have used the word killed in light of Zauditu's disappearance," said Kia.

The Wright brothers waited with Kia some time for Ralph, but he did not show up. Eventually, Kia told them that she had to return to the circus to rehearse and prepare for the evening show.

"I'll see you guys later," she said while leaving the park.

"Bye, Kia," said Havier.

The Wright brothers waited in silence for a few minutes.

"I don't think Ralph is going to show up, Marcus," Havier told his younger brother.

"Let's wait a few more hours, just in case," Marcus said enthusiastically. Apparently Marcus liked looking for people in the park because he had resisted waiting for people at the circus.

"A few more hours? Get out of here with that! How about one more hour and that's stretching it," said Havier.

"Aight," Marcus grudgingly agreed.

The hour passed slowly. About forty minutes into it, Marcus spotted Ralph coming into that area of the park.

"There he is, Havier," said Marcus with an energetic whisper.

Ralph sat down on a bench and seemed to be lost in thought.

"Let's go question him," Marcus said impatiently.

"No. We should give him a minute to get settled. He'll be more likely to speak then," Havier said with caution.

Ralph sat there with his head hung low and his arms resting on his knees. After a few minutes, he stood up and strolled toward the woods with his head hanging low. Most interestingly, he was wearing his magician's outfit. The snazzy suit was a crisp black color and had a tuxedo styled jacket with a split in the back. In his hand he carried a magician's top hat which he swung by his side as he walked.

It was strange to see him in the park with a circus performer's outfit on. No other circus entertainer wore their outfit to the park. Kia, Eric and Jake were always wearing casual clothing when the Wrights saw them outside of the circus.

"He's going in the woods Marcus."

"Let's follow him," Marcus said standing up.

Ralph entered the woods with the Wright brothers close behind.

"He looks like he might be going to the same spot Eric and Jake were talking at," Marcus whispered.

The Wright brothers walked carefully through the woods and crouched down behind the same rock they had hidden behind before. Ralph was sitting there moping.

"I can't believe I did that for the money," he said to himself.

"What's wrong with him?" asked Marcus whispering.

"I don't know," Havier said quietly.

"Well, I hope I get the money soon enough so that I can get my trick. You never know how these things go. I can't take them looking for me anymore," Ralph droned on.

"Is he talking to himself, because I don't see anyone else?" Marcus observed.

"Yes," Havier whispered.

All of a sudden Ralph froze and looked toward the Wright brother's hiding place. He smiled and put the magician's hat he was carrying on his head. Without warning, a bang, followed by a puff of smoke appeared around him.

"Listen for the footsteps Marcus," said Havier.

The crackling of leaves under Ralph's feet served as a tracking device for the Wright brothers.

"He's headed in the same direction Eric and Jake went!" Marcus exclaimed.

Taking off running, the Wright brothers were in hot pursuit of Ralph. As the detectives passed the smoke, they caught sight of Ralph.

"There he is Havier!" Marcus yelled while trying to catch his breath.

All of a sudden a loud bang, followed by another puff of smoke appeared and concealed Ralph.

"He's entering the path! Which way do we go?" Marcus asked.

"Go left and I'll go right. If you see him, yell for me. If you don't see him meet back here in sixty seconds.

Marcus ran down the path toward the left counting the seconds as he ran. After thirty seconds, he turned around and ran back to the spot where they had exited the woods. Havier was also running back with perfect timing. On the other side of the path that they ran down, opposite of where they had exited the woods, was a hill covered with thick brush.

"Let's go up that hill. He can't have gotten far," said Havier.

The Wright brothers were in great shape and were able to scale the hill with amazing speed.

"There he goes!" Marcus exclaimed when the two brothers got to the top of the hill. The hill sloped down into another wooded area with fewer trees.

"He's running that way!" Havier yelled as he saw Ralph fly thorough the forest below them.

The Wright brothers ran down the hill and chased after Ralph. Then a large bang and puff of smoke appeared behind the magician.

"Don't let him get away, Havier!" Marcus yelled.

As soon as Ralph became visible, another cloud of smoke concealed him again. The Wright brothers stayed on Ralph's heels despite the difficulties with the smoke clouds. Ralph ran without looking back.

"We're gaining on him, Hav! We almost got him!" said the youthful Marcus.

"Keep running and we'll catch him!"

After a few more minutes of the chase, the woods came to an end. They opened into a large grass field that was at least the size of a football field, but probably bigger.

"We got him now!" yelled Marcus.

Ralph was approaching the center of the large field. The Wright brothers were close behind him. It looked as though they would certainly catch him before he reached the other side of the field. All of a sudden Ralph stopped in the middle of the field. He rotated his arms in a circular fashion. Several large booms occurred all throughout the field. There were about eight clouds of smoke that appeared. However, this time they were blue and all were about twenty yards apart. None of the clouds concealed Ralph, and not one of them disappeared right away like the white clouds of smoke. Instead, the blue clouds seemed to be made out of a thicker type of smoke that just stayed in one place. On top of this, the wind was not blowing that day so the clouds of smoke just sat there in the field.

"Get him!" Havier told Marcus.

"He won't get away now!" Marcus replied.

The Wright brothers were almost upon the magician. A few more seconds and they would have him.

With his back turned to the Wright brothers, Ralph levitated about a foot off of the ground. Then a big bang was followed by a big puff of white smoke which surrounded him. Havier and Marcus stopped abruptly about twenty-five feet from the smoke puff.

"You go left, I'll go right and well meet in the middle on the other side. Any way he runs we'll see him for sure. Yell if you've got him and I'll be there," Havier instructed his younger brother as he ran to the right.

Marcus and Havier ran all the way across the field making two big semicircles. Except for moments when they passed behind clouds of blue smoke, they could see one another clearly as they ran through the field. They met on the other side of the field and kept looking across the field for Ralph, but they were dumbfounded. The blue clouds of smoke had begun to thin out, and they could pretty much see through them. It seemed as though Ralph had disappeared into thin air. He was nowhere in the field, and it was impossible for him to have escaped from such a wide open space. The clouds of smoke only covered small sections of the massive field and the Wright brothers covered every angle of the field as they ran across it.

"Ralph was ghost. He just disappeared in thin air," said Marcus.

"I can't believe we were so close, but so far," said Havier.

"What should we do now?"

"Well we're on the other side of the field. So I think we should walk back across, leave the park and return to the circus."

"Do you think Ralph is going back to the circus today?"

"Quite possibly, especially if he calls Kia. She will tell him that we were there once today and that we probably won't be coming back."

The Wright brothers grudgingly walked across the field, stopping periodically in disbelief that they had missed Ralph. As they paused, they looked in several directions across the field, hoping that Ralph would emerge from some hiding spot in the woods. This constant stopping and talking resulted in a twenty minute walk across the field. When they got across, they walked back through the woods, passed the pond, by the park goers, and exited the park. During the subway ride, they were both solemn and quiet. The Wright brothers felt as though they had lost an important opportunity to locate Zauditu.

Chapter 16: A Motive for the Crime

Hoping that Ralph foolishly went back to the Black circus, the Wright brothers entered the arena. They headed for Ralph's tent, but he was nowhere to be found.

"Great what do we do now?" asked Marcus.

"Well we can hang around for a little while. We also have some more leads to investigate," Havier replied.

"What do you mean Hav?"

"Well, the way I see it is just this. Who was in the tent when Zauditu disappeared?"

"Eric and Mary or possibly Jake," answered Marcus.

"Right, so far we've found out information on Jake and Eric when we followed them in the park. We have information about Ralph and, depending on the DNA results, we might have some evidence against both Ralph and Jake. But Mary was probably in that tent when Zauditu climbed out from under the Elephant."

"But we spoke to Mary already and she didn't say anything about Zauditu. She was all wigged out. Next to Jake, she has been the least helpful of all of the people we have spoken to."

"Yeah, but remember Marcus that we were able to find out things about Jake by following him. So we might have to use other means to find out information from Mary."

"So, you think we should follow Mary?"

"Not yet. I think we should use other means."

"Like what?"

"Investigative means," Havier replied while sounding as though he was stalling.

"Investigative means? Like what?" Marcus pushed.

Havier avoided answering, "Let's go talk to the circus managers again. It's been a while since we spoke with them. They might have noticed something important. Then we can slip in questions about Mary and the other circus employees when we get the chance."

"Aight."

The Wright brothers headed to the circus management's office.

"Excuse me sir," said Marcus to a short Black man who answered the door. "We had a few questions about the disappearance of Zauditu."

"Come on in and have a seat. My name is Mr. Freeland," said the man.

Havier introduced himself, "Hi, I'm Havier Wright and this is my brother Marcus. We previously spoke to another member of your management team. We're investigating Zauditu's disappearance."

Mr. Freeland was wearing a neatly pressed tuxedo. "Yes, yes they told me that you guys would be here. You two are helping your father write a story on Zauditu's disappearance. I hope you're able to write a good story about this case," he said.

"Yes, well we were wondering about Mary..." Havier was cut off by Mr. Freeland.

"She was good friends with Zauditu. The poor woman was so disturbed by Zauditu's disappearance. I was so worried that she might not be able to continue with her act here at the Black circus. But she seems to have rebounded very quickly. She's in good spirits now," Mr. Freeland explained.

"I'm glad to hear that," said Havier in a conversational tone.

"Zauditu and Mary were so close that she listed Mary as a beneficiary on her official circus employment forms. She even has Mary down as the recipient of her life insurance policy. Mary was closer to Zauditu than most of Zauditu's family. Some of Zauditu's family members weren't too happy about Mary being the recipient of the policy," said Mr. Freeland.

"Zauditu had a life insurance policy?" asked Marcus.

"That's right. But it's not unusual for circus performers to have a life insurance policy. In fact, many of my performers have a life insurance and injury insurance policy. If I remember correctly, Zauditu had a $1,000,000 life insurance policy. A lot of accidents can happen in a circus. Some circuses even lose performers for good."

"Have you guys ever lost a performer? I mean for good?" asked Marcus while swallowing.

"No, and I don't intend to. I always say that safety comes first and I expect that whoever kidnapped Zauditu will return her," explained Mr. Freeland.

"During the day of her disappearance, did anyone in the circus act strangely before or after the show?" asked Havier.

"Not that I can remember. It was business as usual. I've got a lot of employees you know, and I can't keep track of how all of them are feeling and acting every day."

"What about in the days after the show. No one acted funny at all? What about Mary? Did she say anything or do anything out of the ordinary?" Marcus pressed the issue.

"As a matter of fact, I heard Mary talking to Eric about going back home to Ethiopia. She said something about…" Mr. Freeland paused, "Now let's see, if I remember it right she said that all this was over and that she was going to go back to Ethiopia to buy a large home. Yep, that's what she said. I figured she was sad about Zauditu and just wanted to go back home. But then again, I overhear talk like that from circus performers all the time and they don't really mean it. You know it's very lonely here at times," explained Mr. Freeland.

"I see," replied Havier.

Mr. Freeland continued, "You know she had just lost her best friend Zauditu, poor woman. I wish I could have done something to cheer her up."

"But she's feeling better now right?" asked Marcus.

"Yes, Eric said he talked to her in the days following Zauditu's disappearance. By the next week she was back to her normal chipper self."

"That sounds like a quick recovery," Havier observed.

"Yes, it was. I'm very thankful for what Eric did. I probably would have lost Mary. I mean she already wanted to leave the circus before her best friend disappeared. Just imagine how she felt after she lost her best friend. That would make me want to leave, even though I love the circus."

"Is there any reason that she did not leave yet?" Havier asked.

"Right after Zauditu disappeared, Mary told us she would almost certainly be leaving the circus. Mary said she was waiting on something important before she left. I left it alone because of her state of mind," Mr. Freeland explained.

"Has she said anything more about when she is going to leave?" Marcus queried Mr. Freeland.

"No, and I'm happy it's that way. Do you know how hard it is to find a replacement for someone like Mary? I know that she won't be here much longer, but I certainly appreciate every minute that she's here. Plus, her staying gives me a little more time to find a replacement."

Havier wanted to double check on the whereabouts of everyone during the crime. While he had been told Kia's whereabouts by another manager, he wanted to make sure her story, and everyone else's were correct.

"Do you know where Eric, Mary, Ralph, Jake and Kia were during Zauditu's disappearance?"

"Let's see, that's a good question. Ralph was on the floor in front of the crowd doing magic tricks. Kia was also on the floor the whole time. Jake was tending to the animals in his tent. Eric and Mary were on the floor for part of the time, and then they went into Jake's tent to give him a break. You know, they were getting the last few elephants and horses into Jake's tent for him. Those folks really help to hold this show together. They're great," Mr. Freeland said praising his employees.

"Is there anything else you can remember that seemed out of the ordinary when Zauditu disappeared?" Marcus asked in a last attempt to find out more information.

"No, that's about it. I just hope the police are able to locate Zauditu. We really miss her here at the circus," Mr. Freeland said compassionately.

"We do too," Havier agreed.

"Take care Mr. Freeland," said Marcus.

"You two young men be careful."

"We will," the Wrights replied together.

Havier and Marcus left the management office. Much of the information provided by Mr. Freeland confirmed their worst fears.

Chapter 17: A Revealing Conversation

While the Wright brothers had not been able to locate Ralph, they had come upon a wealth of information from their conversation with Mr. Freeland. They felt like there was now a motive for Zauditu's disappearance. A life insurance policy of $1,000,000 was a lot of money. Before they left the circus they thought that it would be a good idea to try to see if they could photograph the trampolines and their trap doors for evidence. On the way to the tent which stored the trampolines, they passed the tent that Eric shared with a few other clowns and heard a voice coming from inside.

"It's too bad Mary, too bad," said Eric in a saddened tone.

"Yeah, well you know she's gone now and I'm getting the insurance money. I'm going back home Eric and I'm going to live my life. I am going to live my life in peace away from the circus forever," said Mary.

"What about my part?" asked Eric.

"Of the money?"

"Yeah, and then there are the other three. Don't you think they deserve some of that money too?"

"Maybe, maybe but I'm not sure if they should get an equal amount," explained Mary.

"Not sure? They were our partners in this venture. They stood by our side through thick and thin and you're just going to cut them off like that?"

"I don't know Eric, that's my money and I have plans."

"No, that's our money. All five of us deserve an equal share. You wouldn't even have that money if I didn't convince Zauditu to take out an insurance policy. I was the one who got her to take it out and I expect a fair share," argued Eric.

"Just remember Eric, just remember that there's not a dime coming to me unless Zauditu's body turns up," said Mary and then she broke out crying.

"Don't worry, it will all be worked out. You'll have your money soon and you'll be back home away from this mess."

"And then there are those two teenagers snooping around here," she said sobbing.

"I know, they're starting to get annoying, but they don't know much. Jake said that they tailed him a couple of times. He said he got so nervous that he had to climb a tall fence. I told him not to run from them anymore because it makes him look suspicious," explained Eric.

"So how would you handle them if they approach you?" Mary sniffled between words as she asked her question.

"That's a good question because you don't want to put some kind of spotlight on yourself when you don't have to. I would just be nice and give vague answers. And when I say vague, I don't mean the answers you were giving right after Zauditu was carted out of this place. I mean clear and concise answers that don't really reveal much," explained Eric.

"I know what you mean Eric. It's just hard for me."

"Well, if they question you and you get in some uncomfortable situation then you can just tell them that I might be able to answer their question better than you can. Don't slip up, Mary. If they find out it'll be over for us," Eric warned Mary.

"If they ask personal questions about Zauditu, I might just break down and tell them everything about the insurance policy, the bloody knives and all the other stuff."

"Don't do that! Don't do that! Because if you do that it might mean the end of all of us."

"I don't know about this. All I know is that I just want to go home. I'm tired of the questioning. I'm tired of the circus and Zauditu is gone," she said weeping again.

"Look Mary, just stay on the straight and narrow. And we'll be out of here in a couple of weeks."

There was silence in the tent for about fifteen seconds. Then Eric and Mary walked out of the tent. Havier and Marcus were standing there looking rather stupefied. Mary and Eric were surprised to see them.

"Hi, guys. Did you two just get here?" Eric asked nervously.

Realizing the gravity of the situation, Havier avoided Eric's question without lying, "We were in the office speaking with Mr. Freeland. We came over this way to check out some of the circus equipment."

Havier's crafty answer alleviated many of Eric and Mary's fears. Eric thought that Havier and Marcus had just arrived at his tent, but he was still slightly worried that his and Mary's conversation had been overheard.

"Oh well, good luck," said Eric.

"By the way, have you seen Ralph lately?" asked Marcus.

"No, I haven't seen him all day. In fact, I haven't seen him for a couple of days," said Eric.

"Me neither," Mary added.

"Maybe if you check back another day he might have returned," Eric thought out loud.

"You think so?" asked Marcus.

"Yeah, he's bound to be back before the first show next weekend," Eric explained.

"Are they going to put him back in the circus?" asked Havier.

"That depends on whether Zauditu is found. You know the circus management isn't going to allow its acrobats to disappear until this whole Zauditu thing is resolved," said Eric.

"Well, we hope she's found soon," said Havier optimistically.

"So do we," Eric replied insincerely.

"We're going to check out some of the other stuff here at the Circus," said Havier.

"You two take care," said Eric trying to sound compassionate.

"You, too," Marcus replied.

The Wright brothers continued on to the tent with the trampolines. They took several pictures of the trampolines with the trap doors. After taking the pictures, they exited the circus and traveled home. They had much more to discuss. Mary was now a prime suspect in the case. Zauditu's disappearance was beginning to look even more complex. It appeared as though at least five people were involved in the crime. Who was guilty? And who had no role in the affair? Both brothers knew what it was like to be wrongly accused, and despite Marcus' testiness, they didn't want to wrongly accuse any of the circus performers without conclusive evidence.

Both detectives were quiet during their ride home on the train. After Havier and Marcus arrived at home, they ate dinner. Their amazing silence showed a tremendous amount of discipline as well as preoccupation with the case. After eating, the two detectives went into the living room and turned on the news.

The reporter announced, "The case of the disappearing acrobat just became more troublesome. Late tonight, circus officials received a letter demanding ransom for the acrobat's return. It is not clear whether the acrobat is alive or not. However, the note demanded $1,000,000. What is also not clear is how the circus will generate these funds to pay for the safe return of the acrobat."

"You hear that! A ransom note! I bet it's Ralph's note. Remember he wanted that money for the magic trick!" Marcus exclaimed.

"Let's not rush to conclusions Marcus. Hold on, let me hear the rest of the news report," Havier said.

"The ransom note was mailed to circus officials and they opened it tonight. Here is what one of the managers had to say about it."

"Hey, that's Mr. Freeland," said Marcus.

"I just hope that we can get her back soon. The only problem is the money," said Mr. Freeland on the news.

"There was one more point of interest. The ransom note was signed: 'The Duplicitous Five.' The police still have to determine what this means," the reporter concluded.

"Eric and Mary spoke about three others today. Matching that with what we just heard, that could mean that five people were involved in the kidnapping. Let's see: Ralph, Jake, Eric and Mary, that would be four of them and there must be one other person involved. It's probably someone we don't suspect, like Kia or something," Marcus thought out loud.

"Marcus you can't jump to conclusions. I told you that jumping to conclusions without evidence is not the way to go. Evidence my brother, proof is what we need. And Kia has been the most helpful person at that circus. Don't start accusing people who you don't have any evidence against at all. The management told us that Kia was on the floor during the whole circus and the disappearance," Havier enumerated.

"So was Ralph," Marcus countered. "But I got what you're saying. I'm not going to accuse someone in front of the police if I don't have the right proof. I don't agree with that, especially after what we went through with those White cops. But we have to work things out for this case and sometimes we might think it's someone even if we don't have any evidence against them."

"I know but any one of them might have been involved. It's all about the evidence. I'm just bothered about the note and ransom money. Especially after the conversation that we heard between Mary and Eric today," Havier stated.

"True but you know that they probably did it," Marcus pushed.

Havier gave an unwilling nod which let Marcus know that he mostly agreed with him. After the conversation concluded the Wright brothers used the rest of the evening to complete all of their homework for the next week. They had a long week of school ahead of them before they could continue some serious sleuthing next weekend.

Chapter 18: An Attempted Mugging

The week passed quickly. Both Marcus and Havier aced quizzes and exams in their classes. Marcus received a ninety-eight on a math quiz. Havier obtained a ninety-five on his English exam. By Friday, the Wright brothers were ready to get back into investigating the case.

The upcoming weekend marked the start of the fourth weekend that the circus was in the city. The circus would only be in town for two more weeks. The Wright brothers felt a deep sense of urgency to solve the case. They planned to question Ralph on Saturday. He was bound to have returned to the circus by then.

Every night of the week, they made sure to check the news report for breaking stories on the case. Friday night was no exception. Besides the normal report that Zauditu had not been located, it contained some exciting information about the case.

"A suspect in the disappearance of the acrobat from the Black circus has been identified by the police department. Apparently, the acrobat's DNA has been found on a knife containing her blood and the suspect's fingerprints. The police declined to name the suspect. Apparently the suspect is at large. The police will release a name and description of the suspect some time tomorrow," said the reporter.

"Wow! That's Ralph!" Marcus exclaimed.

"I guess they've got him," said Havier.

"Not yet."

"Yeah, they'll probably have him soon if they can find him."

"Oh, they can find him. You better believe that Havier," Marcus said conclusively.

"Maybe," Havier said doubting his younger brother.

"So what do you think we should do to help further the case along?"

"What should we do? Marcus, the police are able to catch Ralph one, two, three. He's caught and we're done."

"He's caught and we're done, but what about the other people involved in the kidnapping?"

"Well, we got about all we're going to get out of them. You know Jake is just running from us and you heard Eric and Mary last weekend. They plan to divert any conversation that we have with them and to talk about nonsense," Havier enumerated.

"But what about…" Marcus started.

Havier interrupted him sounding annoyed, "What do you want to do, go speak to Kia again?"

"Actually that idea might work, but I actually had another thought."

"Like what?"

"The circus stores; I keep having this feeling like the circus stores have some more evidence. Maybe they have some more knives. Maybe they have something else. But I know that we need more proof to accuse the others. Plus I would really like to go and speak with Eric. There's something about that conversation in the park that I didn't like."

"I don't know about that, Marcus. If Jake's hook comes back with Zauditu's DNA on it, then we will have enough evidence against him. And whether Eric is involved in the crime or not, I really don't care," Havier said.

"But we don't have enough proof against Eric or Mary. All of that evidence is circumstantial. I know that we might be able to get some more out of Eric. He did say that he would be nice and speak to us. Remember, he tried to say that he would cover up everything. Plus, the circus store has some other evidence. Mr. Brunson opened his whole store to us and you don't want to go through it? Maybe a more careful search would help," Marcus said passionately.

"That takes a long time."

"Peep this. We could start today and finish tomorrow or at the latest, next weekend. Maybe we could spend some time talking to Kia tomorrow, if we got the chance," Marcus replied.

"Well it sounds kind of far out, but I'm down."

The next day the Wright brothers headed over to *Party Hardy Now and Circus Enterprises* to see Mr. Brunson. Upon arrival in the afternoon, Mr. Brunson was seated behind the counter on the fourth floor.

"Hi, Mr. Brunson," Havier said with a smile.

"Hi, Havier," Mr. Brunson responded.

"We wanted to look through some more of the items purchased by the Black circus," said Havier.

"Did you guys see the news last night? The police are hot on the trail of a suspect. They said something about a DNA match with Zauditu's DNA. I hope those knives you fellows took on out of here and gave to the police weren't the knives they were talking about on the news because that would be real bad for Ralph the magician. He's a good guy, but those were his knives that I gave you and there's not much he could say to the police if they had Zauditu's DNA on them."

"Yeah," Havier grudgingly agreed.

"We'd like to take a look at the other items, if possible," Marcus redirected the conversation.

"Sure, but do you think that Ralph was the only one involved?" Mr. Brunson asked.

Havier tried to avoid giving a direct answer to the question, "We're still collecting evidence. We really can't make any judgments about people. That's the job of the those who look at the evidence."

Mr. Brunson gave them the inventory list and said, "I wish you guys luck."

"Thanks, Mr. Brunson," Havier replied.

The Wright brothers spent several hours combing through the circus inventory. However, they did not come across anything that seemed useful. They looked at circus batons. They looked over unicycles and harnesses for the animals. Even after a few hours of looking, they did not come close to going through the entire list. In fact, the tedious process made them edgy and they decided to leave the store. The Wright brothers returned the list to Mr. Brunson and headed over to the other circus store that Jake had gone into.

Upon their arrival at the stop near the store Havier said, "Here is what I think we could do when we go to the store. Stay on the low, look through the items, and then we'll question the managers. If there are a lot of people in there, we'll blend in while we're looking through the items. Then we'll buy what we want and question the managers. If they don't want to answer questions about the inventory, then we'll be out."

"Aight," replied Marcus.

The Wright brothers quickly scanned through items in the other circus store for a few minutes, but they were unable to find any items of interest.

"Let's go ask the manager some questions," said Marcus.

The manager on duty was the same tall, lanky White man who was there before. He was talking to another manager who was a short, heavyset Caucasian.

"Excuse me, sir," said Havier, "we had one or two questions."

"Yes how can I help you?" the manager said while trying to continue his conversation.

"I wanted to know if anyone from the Black circus ordered any items that might have been out of the ordinary?" Havier asked.

"If we could see an inventory that would be great," Marcus added.

"The tall skinny manager was still staring into space, but suddenly looked at Marcus. "Hey, you two were here before!" the man said angrily.

"Well…" Havier paused.

"Look, do you know how absurd your question is? I need you to get out of this store and don't come back. Ever again!" the man shouted.

"But we were just…" Marcus started.

"No, you were just leaving," said the short heavyset manager as he motioned toward the door of the store.

The Wright brothers walked solemnly toward the door. Not only had they lost the future opportunity to review the store's items, they might have permanently ruined their ability to uncover evidence pointing to other suspects. After they exited the store, they quietly walked down the block for a few minutes.

"That sucks!" said Marcus when they were far away.

"Want to go to the park and cool out?" Havier asked trying to calm down his younger brother.

"Aight, let's walk."

Central Park was a couple miles walk from where the Wright brothers were. However, both of the sleuths were up for the walk. They sort of lollygagged as they walked down the streets of Manhattan so that they got to the park in a little over an hour. They walked through a busy area of the park to a section in which few people could be seen hanging out. This was a different area of the park that they had never walked through. The area had a clearly defined path, but woods bordered both sides of it. Continuing their stroll, the Wright brothers walked slowly through the park.

"It'll be dark in about an hour or so Marcus. So let's try to be out by then," said Havier.

"Ok," said Marcus.

"It's too bad we got kicked out of that circus shop," Havier noted.

"Well, it's not the end of everything. The police will probably have Ralph in their custody soon. Plus we can go to the other circus store any time and Mr. Brunson will help us out."

The Wright brothers walked and talked for some time. They noticed other park goers heading for the exits of the park and decided that it would be a good idea to leave the park in a few minutes. The place they had entered was about fifteen to twenty minutes away, depending on how fast they walked.

They talked about the case for about ten more minutes. The conversation was so engaging that they didn't notice that dusk had set in and virtually all of the park visitors had left.

"Let's go, Marcus," said the more responsible Havier.

"Ok."

About a minute or two into their exit, they realized that someone was following them. He was a medium sized, well-built man.

"Look, Havier, that guy is following us."

"Just keep walking," replied Havier.

"We should walk faster."

The Wright brothers quickened their pace.

"He's walking faster," whispered Marcus with tension in his voice.

"Just keep going. We'll be out of here in a few minutes," Havier said trying to comfort his brother.

"What's that in his hand?"

"I don't know. It's shinny and looks like a knife."

"I think we should jet!" Marcus said with urgency.

"On three, we'll run. One, two, three!" Havier said while he and his brother took off running.

"He's going to catch us," said Marcus after about two minutes of running.

"Keep running," Havier said breathing heavily.

Havier and Marcus bolted down the park pathway at top speed. The park was empty and complete darkness was about to set in.

"Run, Marcus!" Havier yelled.

There was a strange silence from the man chasing them. He was almost like a ghost. But this man was real.

"He's about to get us," Marcus said when they were about three minutes from the park's exit.

"Run Marcus! Run!" Havier said again.

The man had been about one block behind the Wright brothers at the start of the chase. Now he was only seventy-five feet away and quickly closing on the sleuths. The Wright brothers continued to run as fast as they could and the man got closer and closer.

"Just a little bit more and we're out!" Havier exclaimed.

The Wright brothers ran towards the exit to the park. Havier glared at the man. He was only twenty feet behind them, but was gaining rapidly. The Wright brothers dared not look back any longer. Instead, they ran for the park exit.

Just then, the man grabbed Marcus and pressed the knife to Marcus' face.

"Give me all of your money!" the man shouted.

"Ok, it's in my pocket," Havier responded.

"Get it!"

Havier reached in his pocket and tossed his wallet to the man. The man momentarily released Marcus to catch the wallet and Havier ran at the man and tackled him. The man lost his balance, hit the ground and dropped the wallet.

"Ouch!" the man yelled as he clutched his head.

"Marcus, let's go!" Havier yelled.

Marcus reached down and grabbed his wallet. Then, the Wright brothers bolted toward the park exit.

"We made it, Hav!" Marcus exclaimed as they exited the park. Several people were walking down the sidewalk. Some were quite close to Havier and Marcus when they exited.

"Where did he go?" Havier asked looking back into the park.

"He was right there, but I don't see him anymore."

"Did you get a good look at his face?"

"Not really, I was too scared," said Marcus.

"I got a quick look at his face when he grabbed you."

"Thanks for tackling him. I think he hit his head on the ground or on a rock," Marcus observed.

The Wright brothers looked for a police officer in the vicinity of the park exit, but there were none in the area. As a result, they decided to file a report of the attempted robbery and mugging with Captain James the next day. As they walked to the subway, they both felt both shocked and empowered that they had been able to avoid the mugging.

The train came quickly and both of the Wrights filed onto a subway car that was unusually packed for this time of day. The riders were shoulder to shoulder and the Wrights joined the sardine can back to Brooklyn. The subway stopped a few times with little relief from the crowd. To add to the conditions, vendors and others occasionally pushed their way from one end of the car to the other. Then the subway stopped, somewhere near the village, but not quite in it. Marcus looked to the right of where he was standing. It was Eric!

"Eric! How are you!" Marcus blurted out to the circus performer who had been standing less than a few feet away from them for almost the entire ride.

"Ma, Ma, Marcus?" Eric said with extreme supprise.

"So where are you headed Eric?"

The subway rocked from side to side swaying all of the passengers. Simultaneously some sparks appeared outside of the train.

"Uh, well you know, I'm going to see Jake and some other friends."

"Well we've been meaning to talk to you about the case," said Marcus.

"Oh, well now is a really bad time. I would be happy to speak to you two some other time," Eric said evasively.

"Well we just want to know more about you're involvement in the case."

The train rocked again, this time more violently.

"Well, let's see," Eric said seeming flustered. "I was very upset at the whole incident with the knife, you know."

It seemed as though Eric was getting ready to confess, and Marcus pressed him further.

"We know about the knife Eric. You can tell us what happened. We know all about the blood on the knife and everything."

"You do? Well..." Eric paused momentarily. The subway violently rocked again, but this time the lights flashed, and then went out.

"Ladies and Gentleman we have a temporary electrical problem that will be corrected shortly."

"So Eric, you were about to tell us about the knife."

Silence followed and so Marcus said, "Eric did you hear me."

About ten seconds later the lights turned back on in the train. They hadn't been out more than twenty-five seconds, but Eric was no place to be seen.

"Where did he go Hav?"

"I don't know. I don't see him," the taller Havier said while trying to peer over the packed train car."

Eric was gone. The train stopped at the next train stop and the conductor asked all of the passengers to get off the train and wait for another approaching locomotive. As the subway riders filed out of the train car, the Wrights scanned the crowd frantically for Eric, but had no luck locating him.

"I'm telling you, I don't trust him. I really don't trust him." Marcus said as they rode home.

Chapter 19: A DNA Match

The Wright brothers filed a report with Captain James in the late morning. He told them that it would be very difficult to locate the man who had chased them. Even though they had a police sketch artist reconstruct Havier's recollection of the man, Captain James explained that it was difficult for most witnesses to accurately reconstruct the face of a suspect. Because Havier only saw the man for a second, and didn't remember his face very well, this made the task of reconstruction even more difficult.

They also told the Captain about Eric and the subway incident. He told them that he would have some of his officers speak with the circus performer again. However, his focus was upon catching the suspect for whom he had the most evidence against.

When Havier inquired about the news report about the suspect that had a DNA match, Captain James confirmed that it was Ralph. He assured the Wright brothers that the evidence that they had found was very helpful at identifying the magician. His fingerprints were found on one of the knives containing Zauditu's blood. The other knife was stained with Zauditu's blood, but had someone else's fingerprints.

Havier and Marcus decided to follow through with their plan to visit Kia. Perhaps she could provide some information about additional suspects.

They got to the circus by the end of the first show. Before entering, the Wright brothers agreed that it was not a good idea to discuss what Captain James had told them about Ralph. They waited until Mary and the other performers went to lunch. Cautiously, they approached Kia's tent. She was in there alone.

"Hi guys, come on in. The others went to get a bite to eat," said Kia.

"How have you been Kia?" asked Havier.

"Ok, what's up with you guys?" she asked.

"Nothing much, we were just wondering if you had any more information on the disappearance of Zauditu," said Havier cautiously.

"Nothing more, I've just been doing the circus thing and worrying about Zauditu."

Marcus was quiet. He was growing very impatient. He wanted to tell Kia that the police were looking for Ralph and that his fingerprints and Zauditu's blood were found on the knife. Maybe if he told her, she could give them a clue as to where Ralph was hiding. Then they could go and apprehend him and would be heroes. Maybe she could give them some information about the other suspect that left his or her fingerprints on the knife. Marcus' ego swelled as he thought.

"So," said Havier with caution, "have you seen Ralph lately?"

"No, I haven't seen him. He hasn't returned. That makes more than a week. We don't need two disappearing acts around this circus. That would devastate everyone," said Kia sounding worried.

For Marcus the tension was building. If Kia knew about the bloody knives, then she might reveal where Ralph was staying. She could also be a witness against him in court. And if she knew about Ralph's involvement, she probably also knew who the other suspect was.

"Was Ralph upset when he left last week?" asked Havier calmly.

"Not really. He just didn't come in. He hasn't called either," said Kia.

By now Marcus was almost bursting at the seams. He was desperate to know where Ralph was and he felt that telling Kia about the evidence mounting against Ralph was essential.

In one long, nonstop string of words, Marcus spoke without taking a breath, "Ralph's fingerprints were found on some of the throwing knives he returned to Mr. Brunson in the circus store, and Zauditu's blood was found on them too! We need to know where Ralph is and who else is involved because the police are looking for him!"

Havier gave Marcus a look of horror. Havier knew that one never reveals information like that to an acquaintance of a suspect; even if they are trustworthy. At that moment, it seemed as though Marcus jeopardized the police's ability to capture Ralph.

"How do they know it was Zauditu's blood?" Kia asked.

"They ran some DNA tests. They compared Zauditu's DNA samples that they collected at the beginning of the investigation with the blood on the knives. The tests showed a match with the blood found on two of the knives. It's pretty much an open and shut case, Kia. DNA evidence doesn't lie. We just need to know where Ralph is and if you know of anyone else who was involved in the crime," Marcus confidently explained.

Havier was too shocked to speak.

"Did you say that Zauditu's blood was found on Ralph's throwing knives?" asked Kia.

"That's right!" replied Marcus.

"Hold on a second. Ralph got those knives to work on a new trick with Makeda. She is Zauditu's identical twin sister. Ralph was working on one of those throwing knife acts. The act required Makeda to be strapped down and to have knives thrown at her while she was on one of those spinning wheels," Kia explained.

Havier snapped out of his trance, "Zauditu has a twin sister? Why didn't you tell us she had a twin sister before? And why didn't anyone else mention her? And if she has a twin sister in the Black circus, how come we haven't met her yet?"

"Well, the answer to your last question is that Makeda is back home in Ethiopia. But it's really a long story," said Zauditu.

"Would you mind explaining it?" Havier said sarcastically.

Kia began to detail what happened, "Sure, as I was saying, right when we arrived in New York Ralph tried this new trick. To do the trick, Makeda had to be tied down to a big, upright spinning wheel. Ralph asked Eric to help him out. So Eric convinced Jake to tie her down and put the blindfold on her."

"Now you think Ralph—as magnificent as he's supposed to be— would have practiced throwing the knives long and hard before he put a real person on that wheel. But he hadn't practiced much. He was relying on his previous experience with magic tricks to accurately throw the knives. Anyway, on his first throw, he missed and the knife caught Makeda on the side of her leg. He begged her to try it again. Eric somehow got her to agree and Ralph threw the knife at her a second time. This time it caught her on her arm and cut her even worse. Even though the cut was worse than the first one, luckily it wasn't too bad. Despite all of the blood, she didn't even need stitches. Ralph wiped off the knife haphazardly, and threw it in the box of other knives. Unfortunately, the whole knife throwing experiment had an unintended negative consequence. Makeda, who was new to the circus this year, decided that the work was too dangerous. So she flew home to Ethiopia," Kia explained.

"Does the management know about this?" asked Havier.

"Oh, yeah. They were the first to know. Ralph was instructed not to try any other knife tricks. He was also told not to do any other tricks that would jeopardize the safety of any of the other performers. When Zauditu disappeared under Ralph's smoke clouds, he felt awful. Being temporarily relieved from his circus duties really hurt him and he's been so down and out ever since."

"Well that explains some of the strange behavior of Jake, Ralph and Eric, but not all of it. Did the management tell anyone about the incident?" asked Marcus.

"Oh no, there was a big cover up. We were asked not to say anything to the media because it would have meant bad publicity for the circus. I guess that's why I didn't tell you anything about Makeda. We all sort of pushed her to the back of our minds."

"Well I understand that Zauditu and Makeda have an exact DNA match, but there were two knives with their blood on them," said Havier astutely.

"Maybe some of the blood dripped off of the first knife onto the second knife." Kia thought out loud.

"That might be true. The only problem is that someone else's fingerprints were found on the second knife," explained Havier.

"Whose fingerprints? Only Ralph touched those knives," said Kia sounding surprised.

"The police don't know yet," said Havier.

"Wow, I hope that this mystery is resolved soon," Kia said.

"So you don't know where we might find Ralph or whose fingerprints were on that other knife?" Marcus pressed.

"Your guess is as good as mine, guys."

"What about Eric. We really need to speak to him."

"No I haven't seen him."

"Thanks, Kia. We have to get going," Havier said abruptly.

The Wright brothers headed over to the management office before they left. Mr. Freeland was inside and invited them in.

"How can I help you guys?" Mr. Freeland asked.

"Actually, we had a question Mr. Freeland," explained Havier.

"What is it?"

"We were wondering if you know about Makeda and the incident," Havier asked him in a leading way to see if Mr. Freeland would independently verify Kia's claim.

Mr. Freeland took a deep breath and spoke, "You must mean the knife throwing incident with Ralph. Oh, we were very embarrassed about that, but I guess it won't hurt to talk about it now. Ralph had Eric tied Makeda down to a vertical spinning wheel and then he threw knives at her. Even though she had agreed to help with the trick, she felt the circus was too dangerous and flew back home to Ethiopia. Poor woman, she was so new to the circus. The other managers and I wanted to avoid a media frenzy so I told everyone to be quiet about it. I guess it doesn't matter now because the circus is suffering so badly from Zauditu's disappearance."

"Thanks, Mr. Freeland. If you tell the police, it might help them find Zauditu," said Marcus.

"Sure, I'll speak to them as soon as I get a chance. The circus is a flop with Zauditu gone and we will be forced to shut it down permanently if she isn't found," said Mr. Freeland sadly.

"I hope they find her soon. Take care Mr. Freeland," Havier tried to comfort him as they exited the office.

"Take care," said Mr. Freeland.

After going to the Circus, the Wright brothers felt that they had to reevaluate the old evidence and examine the new evidence just presented to them. They headed home, both in deep thought and trying to figure out where they should go from here.

Upon their arrival at home Mr. Wright greeted his sons. "Hi, sons, how is your case coming along?" he asked.

"Pretty good, Dad. We were hot on the trail of a suspect, but now we found out he didn't do it," Marcus said.

"Well, just be careful. You can help the police, but let the police do their job."

"Ok, Dad," said Marcus.

At that moment, Mrs. Wright came out of the other room. "Hi Havier and Marcus!" she said.

"Hi Mom."

"I was just telling them to be careful and to let the police do their job."

"Yes, be very careful guys. You don't want to get hurt unnecessarily. Remember to call one of us if you are in a dangerous situation. But please try to avoid getting into trouble with some criminals," Mrs. Wright advised.

"That's a good idea. We have some important information to give to Captain James tomorrow. It's about the DNA evidence in the case," Havier added.

After speaking to their parents, the Wright brothers tried to relax and read. However, their minds were preoccupied with the case. During the early evening, they watched some television. All of a sudden, a newsflash interrupted the programming.

"We have breaking news in the disappearing acrobat case," said the reporter. "The police apprehended the suspect that they were looking for about an hour ago. They have not revealed the identity of the suspect. However, the police have a weapon with DNA evidence linking the suspect to the acrobat. More information will follow on the eleven o'clock news," the reporter concluded.

"Did you hear that! They've arrested Ralph! We've got to go tell Captain James he didn't do it. Right now!" said Marcus.

"Let's go!" Havier exclaimed as he stood up and headed to the front door.

Marcus followed him.

Chapter 20: Clearing Things Up

After hearing the news report that the police had custody of Ralph, the Wright brothers headed to the precinct. The Wrights let the front desk officer know that they were there and took a seat on two chairs that had been placed over to one side of the large room.

Within a few minutes of announcing their presence to the Black officers at the front desk, Captain James emerged from the back of the precinct. As he opened the door to the precinct he held it open for a heavyset white officer. He had graying hair and carried a brief case. He was wearing an unusually dressy police uniform that was decorated with several different pins.

"Take care now sir," said the Captain.

"I'm very proud of you son and the work that you've done on this case," the man said in reply.

"Thanks sir."

"We'll I'm going to get headed back to central. There are a lot of other cases that I have to get briefed on. The acrobat case isn't the only one you know."

"Yes sir I know."

The man hurriedly walked toward the precinct exit and disappeared through the doors.

Captain James paused momentarily. Then he looked up and over in the direction of the Wrights. Smiling he said, "They didn't tell me it was you two who were here to see me. I didn't even know your were sitting there. I just got done meeting with the Chief of police."

"That was the Chief of police who just left?" asked Marcus

"Yes sir, that was the police Chief for the entire city of New York," said Havier.

"He seemed a little agitated," Havier observed.

"Yes he has his moments, but overall he has gone along with the changes that I have implemented here at the precinct. In fact, I just received very good news and I want you two to be the first two outside of the police department to know about it. Ralph was captured at his hotel about two hours ago. He's currently being transported to central booking. In about one or two hours, the arrest will be official. With the District Attorney's support, we should be able to obtain an indictment some time this week," he said confidently.

"Well, we have some bad news Captain James," Havier said with a foreboding tone.

"Yeah, Ralph didn't do it or at least there's a good chance he didn't," Marcus added.

"What do you guys mean?" asked Captain James with concern in his voice.

"Zauditu has an identical twin sister, Makeda. Before Zauditu disappeared, she was part of an act Ralph the magician was trying with those throwing knives. Ralph cut her during practice and returned the knives to Mr. Brunson in the circus store. Makeda decided to go back to Ethiopia because of the incident. The circus management was afraid of the negative publicity, so they covered it up," Havier explained.

"We independently verified the incident at the circus. Kia the clown told us the story and Mr. Freeland, a manager, confirmed it in a separate conversation," Marcus added.

"Hold on a second," Captain James said as he walked quickly to the door leading to the back of the precinct and disappeared momentarily. After about five minutes, he emerged.

"Sorry about that. I had to make a call right away to the detectives handling the case in the Bronx. I told them to put a hold on the official arrest and booking of Ralph because of the information you two just gave me. They're still going to hold Ralph for a few hours until they can independently verify Kia's and Mr. Freeland's stories."

"Thanks Captain James," said Havier.

"You two always seem to be a few steps ahead of the police in this case. You guys are really doing a great job," he complemented the Wright brothers. "Just be careful. Please try not to take it upon yourself to do anything too dangerous."

"The only problem is that we will have to start over from scratch because there is no solid evidence against Ralph," said Marcus.

"Welcome to the world of law enforcement," said Captain James.

"The circus is only in town for two more weekends. Two weeks from today will be their last performance. Then they pack up and are out of town the next day. It won't be long after then that the city and the media forget about Zauditu. As it is, they don't even call her by her name just by 'the acrobat'," Havier asserted.

"You speak with much wisdom Havier. In almost all police cases there is an initial interest period. If an arrest is not made soon, then it can pose a problem for solving the case. We have some cases open for twenty-five or thirty years. Many of them never get solved," said Captain James.

"So how can we speed up the process of capturing the criminals and freeing Zauditu?" asked Marcus with a sense of urgency in his voice.

"The detectives working on this case have made it a top priority. And if you fellows keep doing the great work you've been doing, we just may get a break," Captain James explained.

"Should we keep questioning people and searching for evidence?" asked Marcus.

"Any help you guys can give would be much appreciated, but as I said, be careful."

"Thanks, Captain James," the Wright brothers said simultaneously as they walked out of the precinct.

Havier and Marcus headed home. When they got in the door Marcus spoke first.

"So, where do we go from here?" he asked.

"Well I guess we should look at what Kia told us. We can also look at what evidence still exists," said Havier.

"Yeah, it all fits in now; Ralph being all sad about his inability to participate in the circus because of Zauditu's disappearance. And Eric and Jake's conversation in Central Park about tying her down also makes sense. They were talking about him tying her down to the wheel for the knife trick and nothing more. And then there was the conversation between Mary and Eric. You saw how they acted when we were there. They probably didn't do anything wrong and were just nervous about us hearing about the Makeda incident and the negative publicity the circus would receive," said Marcus.

"Maybe, but remember Ralph also said he couldn't believe he 'did it' for the money. He still may be guilty," Havier said in a balanced tone.

"They probably just didn't want us to know about Mary going home. All of our work is gone."

"Perhaps all is not lost. Anyone of them could have committed the kidnapping. A motive is there for many of them. Mary is still getting Zauditu's money and Ralph needs money for a new trick. Maybe Jake usually rushes around, but that doesn't explain why he and Ralph ran from us. And we know Eric and Mary were in the tent when Zauditu was supposed to climb out from under the elephant. So Eric and Mary could have done it too. Plus there's still a ransom note for $1,000,000 and that amount exactly matches the amount in Zauditu's life insurance policy. Mary is going to get that money and so the motive is there. Anyone of them could have done it," said Havier.

"True that."

"The way I see it is that one of them had to be involved. The only problem is the time crunch to get the case solved."

"Do you think Ralph and Jake might tell us more now that the story about Makeda is out?"

"Maybe, but if they did it, they might be on their guard even more. Plus, if Kia tells Ralph that we were the ones who found the knives in the circus store and turned them in, Ralph might be mad. If he is involved with Zauditu's kidnapping, he might develop a plan to take us out."

"So where do you think we should start?" asked Marcus.

"I don't know, but we shouldn't start with Ralph, Jake, Eric or Mary. That's playing with fire. And remember what Captain James and Dad warned us about. They told us to let the police do their job," said Havier.

"I know we could help out somehow."

"The question is how?"

"How about the circus store? Mr. Brunson is sure to help us out."

"We've been to the circus store and there's nothing more to see. What do you want to see more buttons, unicycles and outfits?" Havier said sarcastically.

"No, but where else are we supposed to go? We could sit by that pond in Central Park until Jake or Ralph or one of the circus people shows up. Or we could look through the stuff in the store that we haven't seen yet. I know it's not much Havier, but maybe we will find something," said Marcus.

"Alright we'll go to the circus store next Saturday."

For the next few hours the Wright brothers watched television. At eleven o'clock they watched the news. The first news story was about Zauditu.

"Earlier this evening we brought you breaking news that a suspect had been apprehended in the case of the kidnapped acrobat. We also reported that a blood stained knife was found containing both the suspect's fingerprints and the acrobat's DNA. However, since our initial report there have been several developments in the case. The police reported that they had to release the suspect because of a problem with the evidence. Apparently, the blood stained knives could not be directly linked to the suspect. Nevertheless, the police have stepped up their efforts to find the missing acrobat and her kidnappers. In fact, they were able to extract some fingerprint evidence from the ransom note," the reporter concluded.

"Wow, more evidence!" said Marcus

"Yeah, more but will it really speed up the process of finding Zauditu?" asked Havier.

"Who knows?"

Chapter 21: Back to the Circus Store

The day was Saturday of the fifth weekend. One week and one day remained before the Black circus would be canceled forever and the city would quickly forget about Zauditu. The Wright brothers decided to head over to *Party Hardy Now and Circus Enterprises.*

"Hi, Mr. Brunson," Havier said when they arrived.

"Hi, Havier and Marcus, how are you doing? Word among the elders is that you two are shaping up to be great detectives."

"Where did you hear that?" asked Marcus.

"From Mr. Collins and you know, Mr. Collins just knows these things," said Mr. Brunson.

"We were wondering if we could take a look at the items that the Black circus ordered again?" Havier asked politely.

"Sure, if you two are here to do some more investigating, I applaud you. Good luck guys," Mr. Brunson said as the Wright brothers went to work surveying the items.

"Havier, do you see anything on the list that stands out?" Marcus asked.

"No, Marcus. I told you before that other than the knives, there isn't a whole lot of important information there," Havier explained with a logical tone.

"Well, I guess we've got to go one item at a time like before," Marcus concluded.

The Wright brothers worked for almost four hours going through the list of items. They went through some of the items they had looked at before and many new items as well. They went through unicycles, bikes, step-up stools, ribbons, replacement trapezes, tight ropes, playing cards, circus hats, circus outfits and megaphones. They looked through horse tassels, decal kits, climbing ropes and lanterns.

With every observation, Marcus became more interested in surveying the items. On the other hand, Havier was more reserved and showed a lackluster interest when looking through the items.

"How much longer do you think it will take?" Havier asked.

"Well, let's see. Probably a few more hours and we will be done," said Marcus.

The Wright brothers worked quietly for the next two hours. Unexpectedly, Havier worked quickly to get the job done. They completed their inventory and examination of the items and Marcus' enthusiasm quickly turned to disappointment.

"See, not a single piece of evidence. All that time and nothing found! What a waste of time!"

Not surprisingly, Havier remained measured and took an optimistic tone, "Maybe, but maybe not my young brother."

"What are you some kind of philosopher?" replied Marcus.

"Nah, I'm just chillin'."

"Let's get out of here!"

"Aight."

The Wright brothers approached Mr. Brunson.

Havier spoke first, "Well Mr. Brunson, we pretty much finished the list. I don't think we'll be back to go through it anymore," said Havier.

"Did you two find anything of interest?" asked Mr. Brunson.

"No, unfortunately not," said Havier.

"Well, maybe if you two come back you will find something."

"Probably not," replied Marcus.

"Thanks for offering, Mr. Brunson," Havier said cordially.

"No problem. You two are welcome here any time," Mr. Brunson responded.

"By the way, you wouldn't happen to have any returned items like the knives that Ralph returned?" asked Havier.

"As a matter of fact, I do! How could I forget? Mary came in and returned a dress she was using in the show. Come on in the back and I'll show it to you."

The Wright brothers walked excitedly behind the counter and into the back.

"There it is," Mr. Brunson pulled out a box containing the dress and opened it.

The Wright brothers inspected the dress carefully with their eyes. They used the grabber to turn it over, but this revealed nothing.

"This dress just looks ordinary," said Marcus.

"That's what I said about the knives until you two sleuths looked at them and saw the dried reddish-brown stuff," responded Mr. Brunson.

"That's true, but it doesn't look like there's anything important about that dress. Was there anything else returned lately by circus workers?" asked Havier.

"No, sorry."

"Please let us know if anyone returns anything else," Havier said kindly to Mr. Brunson.

"Ok. I will."

"See you later Mr. Brunson," said Marcus happily as they left the fourth floor.

The Wright brothers exited the store and decided to head home. It was about 5:45pm when they arrived and the news was about to come on. They were anxious to watch it.

"Good evening. After the disappointing news about the release of a suspect who had been detained, there have been no further developments in the disappearance of the acrobat. According to the circus management, the Black circus will be permanently closing if the acrobat is not found by next weekend. Here is what one circus official said: 'The circus cannot continue under the current circumstances. We hope that she will be found, but it looks bleak.' And that it is bleak," the reporter said as she stopped reading the circus officials comment from a piece of paper she was holding. "Circus officials feel that the negative publicity has hurt the turnout to see them. Audiences are often less than half full. Hopefully, the acrobat will be found."

"We really have to do something, Havier!" Marcus exclaimed after hearing the report.

"Like what?" asked Havier.

"I don't know, but if we don't find Zauditu right away then the circus is going to close," Marcus said with urgency in his voice.

"Well, we are doing all we can. We went through the rest of the list of circus items today. And tomorrow…" Havier paused and seemed confused.

"What are we going to do tomorrow?"

"Actually, I don't know."

"That's what I'm saying, but we have to find Zauditu."

"I'm not sure what more we can do though."

"What about going to talk to Eric, Mary, Jake or Ralph?" asked Marcus.

"That might work, but it also might be bad. We don't know who kidnapped Zauditu. So anyone of them could have done it. Because Ralph was detained, some of them are probably mad at us; especially Ralph. He is probably very angry at us," said Havier.

"Yeah talking wouldn't work much. We could go to the park tomorrow."

"You think so?"

"And sit around? Nah. How about we coup the circus from the outside. We could watch who comes and goes from the arena."

Havier responded, "And where's that going to leave us? It's going to leave us with a nice view of all of the employees going to work and then going home again."

"Probably," said Marcus.

"Let's see. I guess that's it. There's nothing else to do," said Havier.

"How about we look at the pictures we took at the circus again?" asked Marcus.

"We did that already."

"I know but we don't have any leads in the case and just sitting here is a waste of time.

"Most of those pictures are blurry. You can't see anything on them."

"Most of them aren't blurry. Just a few of them are unclear."

"True that, only the one's you took are blurry."

"Only the pictures I took while you were arguing with me are blurry. All of the other pictures are clear," Marcus retorted.

"Well, maybe the clear pictures will have something that we didn't notice before," Havier replied.

"Come on, let's check them out."

The Wright brothers headed into the basement of their home.

Chapter 22: The Clarity of Comparison

After getting settled in the basement, Marcus started the computer that held their pictures. The detectives reviewed the pictures taken in the circus. They looked at each one of them very carefully.

"The problem is that the clear pictures were taken when I wasn't moving the camera," Marcus admitted.

"Yeah all the pictures that were taken during the crime are blurry," Havier said.

"Do you notice anything on the clear pictures?"

"Nothing. I mean I see Kia, Ralph, Mary, Eric and Zauditu in these pictures taken earlier in the show. There's Kia with the picture of a drum on her outfit. In this picture set Mary and Eric are headed towards Jake's tent. That's where they help Jake out with the elephants and acrobats that are hiding under them. Then there's this set of pictures that was taken right when you started to shake the camera. Although they're blurry, I see Kia, Ralph and Zauditu and I assume that Mary and Eric were in Jake's tent by then. Zauditu disappeared during the blurry pictures."

"Do you think Eric was there?"

"Yes because both he and Mary were supposed to meet Zauditu when she climbed out of the tent and several pictures show them walking toward and then into Jake's tent," Havier explained.

"I think it will help if we could be sure that Mary and Eric were in the tent," Marcus insisted.

"How?"

"Well…" Marcus began to reply but was cut off by Havier.

"I think you are just trying to cover up for the fact that you were shaking the camera."

"Not true."

"So what do you think we should do?"

"Let's look at all the pictures again."

The Wright brothers painstakingly reviewed the images that were clear.

"There's nothing here Marcus," said Havier after they looked at all the clear pictures.

"Let's look at the blurry pictures again."

Havier grudgingly complied. The Wright brothers clicked through a number of semi-blurry and blurry images.

Every now and then Marcus would pause and ask, "What's that?"

Havier would say, "I don't know it looks like some of the clowns."

Then Marcus would say, "Oh," and they would keep going. A few minutes would pass and Marcus again would say, "What's that gray blur?"

And Havier would respond appropriately, "It looks like an elephant," or "It's the head of a horse," or "That looks like Ralph the magician and a blurry smoke puff."

After going through quite a few of the blurry pictures, Havier said, "I'm getting tired of this, Marcus."

However, Marcus had a relentless desire to look at each image. "Havier there aren't many more pictures here."

Marcus' enthusiasm got Havier to continue to look at the pictures. However, he kept asking questions that annoyed Havier.

"What's that, Havier?" he asked about one of the trampolines.

"It looks like a trampoline."

"And what's above it?"

"I don't know, it could be a puff of smoke or an acrobat."

"Yeah, it looks kind of blurry. How about this picture Havier? What's that?"

"I don't know, it looks like an elephant," replied Havier sounding annoyed.

"And what's that green thing with a black blotch on it?"

"I don't know Marcus."

"And how about that brown area on the right corner of this picture, what's that?" asked Marcus.

"It's too blurry Marcus! I don't know what it is!" Havier said raising his voice.

"And what about that red blurry thing there by that horse? That could be Zauditu's blood. And look at this one with the trampoline. It looks as though someone is going through the trapdoor. Does it look like that to you, Havier?" Marcus pushed.

"That red thing is probably a clown shoe. Remember all the clowns were dressed in yellow and had red shoes," Havier explained.

"And what's this blurry blue thing?" asked Marcus.

"That's an acrobat's outfit I think. Remember the acrobats wore blue. Look, it looks like that is an acrobat flipping in the air or something," Havier finally added something meaningful to the conversation.

This type of conversation continued until the Wright brothers got through the blurry pictures. The remaining pictures were reviewed at length. However, the Wright brothers were unable to identify anything of interest. Even the final set of clear pictures did not help them.

Finally, Havier said, "Look, all these pictures are clear, but they are of the final clown dance or of Kia and the ring announcer."

Despite Havier's explanation, Marcus was not ready to give up. Even after they looked through all of the pictures during the day that the acrobat disappeared, he still wanted to look at other pictures.

"Let's look at some of the other pictures," said Marcus.

"Which ones?" Havier inquired.

"What about the other pictures we took on our second viewing of the circus."

"Good idea."

The Wright brothers carefully went through all of the pictures that they had taken during their second visit to the circus show.

"Havier that gold thing could be a gun," Marcus pushed.

"That's not a gun. That's a bracelet," Havier explained.

"Oh."

The Wright brothers went through the entire set of these pictures, but they were not helpful because Ralph's act hadn't been in the show they photographed.

Finally, Marcus said again, "There are still more pictures."

"But that's all of them Marcus. What pictures do you want to look at?"

"Let me see, what's on the computer. What about these that Dad took," he said.

"Are you talking about the pictures he showed us that he took when he was testing the camera? I mean the ones of those building rooftops?" asked Havier.

"Yeah."

"Now I know your tripping! You just don't have anything to do!"

"Just move over and I'll look at them," Marcus said while nudging his brother to scoot over so that he could use the computer.

"Aight," replied Havier reluctantly.

"Wow, look at the Manhattan skyline! That's hot!"

Havier did not respond. He realized that Marcus was bored out of his mind and needed something to do.

"And there's the roof Dad showed us," Marcus continued.

"We're wasting time, Marcus," said Havier.

Marcus ignored his older brother, "And there's that rooftop with those guys."

Marcus zoomed closer on the men's heads. Only one of the men was partially turned toward the image. Marcus zoomed in on his face.

"That's hot, right Havier!" said Marcus enjoying the technology at his fingertips.

"Whatever!"

"That eye, Hav. I know I've seen it before."

"Yeah, right," Havier replied sarcastically.

"I knew it! That's where I saw him!" Marcus exclaimed at the top of his lungs. Then he started to move with jerky motions because he was so excited. He minimized the picture he was looking at and clicked another icon on the screen.

"What are you doing Marcus?" Havier asked with interest. But Marcus was consumed with his own anxiety.

"Hold on."

Marcus was clicking so fast that Havier couldn't tell what he was looking for.

"Got it!" Marcus shouted as he continued clicking through another set of pictures.

"Hey that's the..." Havier started to speak when Marcus cut him off.

"That's it! That's it! He's the one who captured Zauditu!" Marcus yelled as loud as he could.

"That's the clown at the school fair! He's the same person that was on that dunking platform! That's the clown who got dunked so many times that he lost his makeup!" Havier exclaimed as he was finally able to get a word in.

"Exactly, look at his shoes Havier. They're the same color as that blurry green patch in the circus. And they have twisted laces too," Marcus explained.

"Hold up. That's a long stretch you're making. You can't really make out the twisted laces in the circus picture," said Havier skeptically.

"But check out the cat on the roof. Look at his face and his eye. That's the same guy who was the clown in the school fair. Look at his face, Havier!" Marcus explained.

Havier examined both the roof image and one of the images from the school fair in which the clown had lost his makeup in the pool.

"Yeah, that's the same guy in both pictures. But you're making a stretch if you think it's the same person who kidnapped Zauditu. I mean green clown shoes are a dime a dozen," Havier poked holes in Marcus' analysis. "And the circus store didn't sell green shoes. The clowns in the circus wore yellow and red; not green. They wore red shoes Marcus. We've been through the inventory and you know that all of the clowns wore red shoes. In fact, no one that I remember wore green in the circus. If they had I would have noticed them in the clear pictures."

"Unless he was just there to kidnap Zauditu. And remember Mr. Collins told us to pay attention to the shapes and colors. I think he was referring to the shoes," said Marcus.

"He could have been referring to a lot of things at the circus store. Connecting those shoes to the circus is still a stretch for me and we'll have to check Mr. Brunson's inventory. Plus anybody could buy a pair of green clown shoes," Havier explained.

Marcus clicked through several of the school fair pictures. One of them was of the clown falling back into the water when he was being dunked. On the bottom of the clown's shoe were small crisp Black numbers. Havier zoomed in as close as he could on the image. The numbers read 10-52 on the bottoms of both shoes. Then he zoomed in on the blurry shoe in the circus. He tried to refine the black portion of the image but was only partially successful, and he still couldn't make out what it was.

"I know it's hard to make out Havier, but the blurry black spot looks like it could be numbers.

"Well maybe, but look where the thing you are calling a shoe is. It's under the elephant," Havier pointed out.

Exactly, this guy dressed up like a clown and kidnapped Zauditu by hiding under the elephant in one of the escape boxes. Because I was snapping so many pictures, I caught his foot popping out of one of the boxes." Marcus explained.

"Ok, but where did he get the shoes? And what do the numbers mean?"

"Let's ask Mr. Brunson tomorrow."

Chapter 23: An Item of Interest

Late Sunday morning, the Wright brothers headed to the circus store where Mr. Brunson worked. They were still in disagreement whether or not he had green shoes in his store. They agreed, however, that Mr. Brunson would certainly have an answer about the green shoes. When they arrived at the circus store, Mr. Brunson had not yet gotten there.

"I know they sell green clown shoes," said Marcus.

"No they don't," said Havier.

Marcus was adamant, "I'm telling you, I know I've seen them here before."

"You can't think rationally about this whole case, Marcus."

"Rationally! Rationally! It was my rational thought that got us to this point Hav!"

"More like your impulsiveness got us here."

"Call it what you want. We were stuck on this case and I opened it wide open!"

At that moment a voice interrupted the Wright brother's conversation. It was that of Mr. Brunson.

"What's all the argument about?" he asked in a warm tone of voice.

"Marcus thinks that you sold a pair of green clown shoes to Zauditu's kidnapper. Is that true? Did you sell a pair of green clown shoes to anyone?" asked Havier.

"The Black circus didn't order any green clown shoes this year. Let me check my extended inventory order list to make sure that someone else didn't order a pair. Hold on a second," Mr. Brunson carefully thumbed through several inventory books. "Yep, yep, I was right. We don't even carry green clown shoes. Don't ask me why because you would think that green is a popular color for clown shoes."

"I knew I was right!" Havier glutted.

"Well, I guess I was wrong," Marcus said remorsefully.

"Thanks Mr. Brunson," Havier said as the Wright brothers left the store.

"No problem, any time," Mr. Brunson said.

Havier and Marcus exited the store.

"So now what should we do?" asked the less than confident Marcus.

"I don't know," Havier replied.

"Maybe we should check the other circus store for the shoes."

"The one we got kicked out of? Are you crazy?"

"Yeah, we could just slip right in and out real quick. If the shoes are there then we would know where they were bought."

"We can't do that B."

"Come on! Let's go!" Marcus said as he marched down the street.

Havier unwillingly complied. When the Wright brothers got to the other circus store it was crowded. They tried to blend in with the customers that were entering the store.

"All of the circus shoes are on that shelf in the back left of the store," Havier said softly as they made their way towards the shoes. Unfortunately, the manager and employee that had kicked them out before were on the other side of the store behind the counter.

"Try to stay low and act normal. Maybe they won't see us," said Marcus as they made their way toward the shoes. "There they are!"

"Yeah, this is the same shoe that was in the images. But now the test," Havier looked at the bottom of the shoe he was holding. It read '9-21'. I wonder what that number means," said Havier.

"Yeah, we should ask an employee."

"No, that's too dangerous."

But Marcus had already gotten the attention of a female employee and began to speak, "Excuse me ma'am, what do these numbers on the bottom of these clown shoes mean?"

"Well, the first number is the size. Like that pair you're holding is size nine. The remaining numbers tell us what pair we sold in that size. They range from 1 to 99 and then we start over at the end of the year. All of our clothing products are stamped this way; shirts, hats, shoes, dresses and pants. The reason we do this is that we offer store credit on all of our products when they are returned. A few years ago customers were returning products that were used and asking for new ones. The majority of people who were doing this were circus employees who came to town for a few weeks each year and got a new pair of clown shoes, pants or some shirts. Stamping the shoes also allows us to do inventory at the end of the year," she said.

"I see," said Marcus.

"So that pair of shoes that says '9-21' is the twenty-first pair of size nine of those shoes that we sold this year," the woman explained.

"But what do these green shoes that say '9-15' mean? These are out of order. It doesn't seem that you sell them in order like: 9-21, 9-22, 9-23," Havier asked.

"That's right, we don't necessarily sell them in order. But usually most of the shoes on the rack have similar numbers. That pair that says 9-15 must have been a return. That's why it's with the 9-20's shoe set."

"What about customers who don't want numbers printed on the bottom of their shoes?" asked Marcus.

"Well, that's not a problem. We get a lot of customers like that. We can remove the ink with a chemical substance similar to nail polish remover. However, when we do that, the customer is forewarned that they may not be able to return the product if there is any wear and tear on it. When they try to return a shoe or other item without a number, we are very careful to make sure that it is in brand new condition before we accept the return.

"Why not just put the numbers on the inside of the shoes?" Marcus asked.

"Good question, because we do that with the clothing labels. The main reason is that it takes too long to do that. Stamping the bottom of the shoes with a number is much easier. It's also a lot easier to see when we do inventory. It takes long enough to look through the other clothes; let alone the shoes.

"After wearing the shoes for a few months, the number on the bottom wears off. And after washing the pants and other clothes several times, the numbers wear off," she explained.

"Could the number come off if it got wet?" Marcus thought back as he remembered that the clown was dunked several times.

"No, water won't take off the ink. You'd have to use a chemical substance like nail polish remover or paint thinner. Either that or you would have to put them in a laundry machine with soap several times or wear them a lot until the number wore off."

"By the way," Havier tried to sound unsuspicious, "would you happen to know who bought a particular pair and color of clown shoes if we gave you the inventory number?"

"No, but the manager over there could help you with that," she said pointing in the direction of the dreaded men behind the counter.

"Thanks," Havier said inconspicuously.

"Your welcome," said the woman.

The Wright brothers quickly left the circus store unnoticed by the managers who had barred them from coming back.

"So, what should we do now?" asked Marcus.

"Let's head to school."

"School, it's Sunday?"

"Yeah, but sometimes the staff comes into work. You know the principal is a workaholic. We might be able to ask them some questions."

"Questions? About what?" Marcus queried his brother.

"Well, we know that the clown shoes link the clown at the school fair to the circus and the possible kidnapping of Zauditu. And we know that that the school knows who he is because they hired him. So we can ask the principal who he is."

"Ok, I'm feeling that."

The Wright brothers headed to their high school. The school was open, but was quite empty. However, the principal was in his office.

"Hello sir, I'm Havier Wright and this is my brother Marcus Wright. We're both students here at the school."

"Yes, I know. Havier you are one of our best students here at the school. Your father is a reporter and photographer. So how can I help you?" said the principal.

"We had a few questions," said Havier.

"What are they?" said the principal.

"Sir, as you know there is an acrobat missing from the Black circus. We are helping our father write a story on the circus and the police have found our leads helpful. We needed some information about the men who were hired for our school fair. Specifically, we would like the names of the clown and his assistant," said Havier.

"Well, I couldn't give you the names of the clown or his assistant even if I wanted to," the principal exclaimed.

"I see," said Marcus in disappointing tone.

"I don't know his name and it's against school policy to give out names of people," explained the principal.

"Well…" Marcus got interrupted by the principal.

"I can, however, give you the names of the companies we hired. They are: 'Magic Flips' and 'Clown Smiles and More.' Magic Flips was the company that provided the games at the fair. Clown Smiles and More provided the whole clown dunking routine. That's all I know. Here are the businesses addresses and phone numbers if you have a question to ask them," said the principal handing them a piece of paper.

"So, these were two totally different companies you hired for the fair?" asked Marcus.

"Yes, as you can see by the addresses, Magic Flips is located in Yonkers, New York and Clown Smiles and More is in Manhattan," the principal explained.

"Thank you, sir," said Marcus.

"No problem, I hope you two make the honor roll this marking period."

"We will," said Marcus.

The Wright brothers exited the principal's office and then the school in silence. When they got outside, Havier glanced down at the addresses.

"Check this out: Clown Smiles and More is located on the same street as the circus store we went to today," said Havier.

"Word?"

"Yeah, it says: '11th floor, suite 102-B' on the address," said Havier.

"Let's check it out," Marcus said.

"Today?"

"Yes."

The Wright brothers headed to the bus that would take them to the train that went to Clown Smiles and More.

Chapter 24: An Unexpected Result

The building containing Clown Smiles and More was slightly down the block and across the street from the circus store. It was several stories taller than the circus store building and contained a fancy lobby, a delicatessen, a music store and a paid parking garage. Having several stores in one building was normal in New York City because the buildings were often very wide and tall. They usually contained many businesses on their upper floors, and sometimes stores took up more than one level. Parking garages were also a normal sight in Manhattan because there wasn't enough parking on the street. People had to pay a half day's wages at a minimum wage job just to park in a lot for a few hours.

"Do you think we should call Dad to let him know that we are going up to this business?" asked Havier.

"Why? We've never called him before," Marcus replied.

"Yeah, but we know that the clown works for this business, and we think that Zauditu was taken by the clown. This could potentially be very dangerous."

"Ok."

Havier called their father, but an answering machine came on. "Hello you've reached Mr. Samuel Wright. Please leave me a message and I'll get back to you as soon as I can."

"Hi Dad, this is Havier. We are on the hot trail of a suspect that kidnapped Zauditu. I just wanted to let you know where we were. I guess you won't get this message until later, but here is the address to the building." Havier left the address of the building and the suite number of the business.

The Wright brothers entered the lobby which contained a security guard who asked them to sign in. After signing the book, they headed to the elevator, entered and pushed number eleven.

"Do you think we should have told the security guard what's happening with this case?" asked Marcus.

"No, we told Dad. He's the best person we could have told," replied Havier.

The elevator quickly climbed to the eleventh floor. The Wright brothers followed the corridor as the hallway signs directed them.

"There are two doors to suite 102-B. Which one should we knock on?" Havier whispered.

"That one looks like the main entrance. Go ahead and knock, Havier."

Havier knocked on the door that Marcus was pointing to. It read: 'Clown Smiles and More,' but there was no answer. He tried the door, but he couldn't get it open.

Marcus nudged Havier and said, "Move out of the way, Havier." Marcus knocked loudly, but he also got no answer. The suspense was increasing by the moment. Then Marcus tried the door and it easily opened. Cautiously, he peered in the office and it appeared to be vacant. He entered the office quietly and Havier followed him.

"It looks empty to me. Maybe they bounced on up out of here," Marcus observed.

The office led to an office to the left, and then to another, and yet another to the left. The Wright brothers followed the corridor-like offices around to the left. All of the offices were sparsely furnished with one desk, one lamp and no visible sign of business activity. There were no scattered papers on desks or pens resting on tables.

"These offices look abandoned," said Marcus.

"Word!" Havier agreed.

All of a sudden they heard what sounded like a door locking in one of the other offices.

"Marcus, that door was locked when I first tried it," Havier whispered.

"And then it was open when I tried it. I was so anxious to get in, I didn't even realize. Havier quick, someone's in here," Marcus warned.

But it was too late.

"Well, well, well what do we have here?" a familiar voice said rhetorically as five men entered the room.

Havier and Marcus were shocked. Five White men stood in front of them. Not only were the clown and his assistant who collected the money at the school fair there, but there were three other familiar men who stood before them. The two Caucasian men who kicked Havier and Marcus out of the circus store were there. Finally, the White man that had followed and chased them through Central Park was standing in front of them.

"In the back!" the tall skinny circus store manager ordered while reaching in his blue and white checkered bag and pulling out a shiny silver weapon. Havier and Marcus recognized this as the same bag in the picture that their father had taken. The man pointed the weapon at the Wright brothers.

The clown and his assistant stood behind Marcus, and the short stocky circus store manager and the man who had chased the Wright brothers through the park stood behind Havier. Now separated, the Wright brothers were forced to walk through a few more small offices until they got to a door. The clown opened the door and the two detectives, and five thugs walked into the room. The Wright brothers were shocked, yet again by what they saw in the next room.

Zauditu was sitting there blindfolded. Her hands were bound to a chair that was bolted to the floor. Her feet were also tied to the chair and her mouth was covered with duct tape. Her head sagged as though she had been unconscious for some time.

The clown removed the blindfold from her eyes. Then he shook her violently and she groggily opened her eyes. It was the first time that she had been awake since they had her bound, balancing in her chair on the edge of the roof. They had contemplated killing her but decided to wait awhile. So instead, they knocked her off the edge of the short wall that surrounded the roof and hit her in the head as she fell. She had been unconscious for some time; maybe for several days, or perhaps a week. Her mouth was dry and her head throbbed.

"Does this look familiar," the clown said pointing to a clown outfit and green clown shoes in the corner of the room.

"Didn't I tell you guys not to meddle in the affairs of the circus store? That should have been a warning enough. And you two come barging in this place like you're trying to investigate," said the tall circus store manager.

"But we didn't know..." said Marcus attempting to find a way out of this situation.

"Untie the girl from the chair so she can walk! Make sure you retie her hands and keep her mouth covered!" the tall manager ordered.

"Let's go," said the short circus store manager.

The clown untied Zauditu and the five men stood behind the three of them.

"Walk!" said the tall circus store manager as the men nudged Havier and Marcus in the back. The Wright brothers and Zauditu unwillingly walked further into the corridor-like office. After passing through two more offices, they came to a door that led to a small room with an elevator. The elevator had a sign which read: *Freight Elevator.*

"Take them up to the roof!" the tall circus store manager barked.

When the freight elevator arrived, they all boarded it and headed to the fifty-fifth floor. Upon arriving, all of the crooks exited the elevator and the Wright brothers and Zauditu were forced ahead. They entered a hallway which led to a door with a stairwell behind it. They were forced to walk up the stairs, through a door and on to the roof of the building.

Once the Wright brothers walked out on the roof, the scene looked extremely familiar. This was surely the roof in the images taken by their father and these five men were the men in those images. With the exception of the small crane that was on the roof in the pictures, it looked exactly the same. This gave the Wright brothers an eerie feeling, but it also made Marcus wonder why the men were wearing construction hats in the picture.

"So, what are we going to do with them?" the clown asked the tall circus store manager.

"This way," he motioned towards the side of the roof opposite of the street. The men pushed the Wright brothers and Zauditu along toward the edge of the roof. A short wall, maybe three and a half feet tall surrounded the roof. The short circus store manager approached Havier and he and the clown's announcer wrestled him to the edge. They pushed the top half of his body onto the wall so that his head was over the building's edge. Havier looked down and swallowed at how far away he was from the ground. The tall manager came over and said, "I told you not to meddle in our affairs. You see that down there, that's where you are going in a few minutes."

Havier gazed down upon the courtyard below. There was a giant thirty by fifteen foot trash bin directly under where the men were holding him. If he and Marcus were pushed in there, they wouldn't survive the fall and might not ever be found.

"Why did you do it?" asked the tall store manager again.

At this moment, Marcus felt compelled to speak up. If they were goners, then at least they would go in dignity.

Speaking to the man bravely Marcus said, "I think the right question is: Why did you guys do it? Why did you kidnap Zauditu from the circus? What did you hope to gain and why did you think that dressing up like a clown and hiding under an elephant would work?"

This caught the men off guard and all five of them turned their attention toward Marcus. This meant that they relaxed their grip on Havier. Havier was impressed by his younger brother's quick thinking. To Havier, Marcus was like that famous Black attorney whom all the famous African-Americans hired to rightfully win their case.

"So, you guys know about the elephant hide away?" the clown started to speak.

"Yeah, when Jake the animal trainer left, he left two of the elephants in his tent for those two stupid clowns who were helping him to bring in the other elephants from the floor."

"You mean Eric and Kia?" asked Marcus.

"Yeah, they were the only two fools in that tent. So while they were talking near the front of the tent, I slipped under the last elephant that was lined up to go out on the floor.

"The original plan was to use my gun to kidnap her. But I realized when I got to the circus that if she decided to struggle, I might be forced to shoot, and this would lead me to get caught in the middle of the circus. So I grabbed a knife from the magician's tent. He had a whole box of them. This actually turned out to be a good move because Zauditu struggled and I would have had to shoot her. The Magician's tent is right next to the animal trainer's tent and so it was easy to slip out of the back of one tent and into another.

"When Zauditu climbed under the elephant, I told her to shut up but she struggled. So I pressed the knife into her arm. As soon as she felt the pain, she complied. I made her climb out in the magician's tent before the elephant entered the animal trainer's tent. These two were waiting on me," the clown pointed to his announcer and the man who had chased the Wright brothers through Central Park. "They took her out of the back entrance of the arena and met them in a van," the clown said pointing to the two circus store employees. "We hopped in the van and made the getaway. Pretty smart, huh!" he said, bragging in an ignorant tone.

"Until you two started asking questions," said the tall circus store employee. "Then I had to send him to tail you," he said pointing to the man who had chased them through the park.

"So you followed us all the way to Central Park from the circus store, and then all the way through Central Park?" Havier said with surprise.

"That's right. I was just waiting until it got dark. I wanted to make it look like a mugging just in case someone else saw or found out. You guys are lucky you got away because that would have been the end of you! I guess it really doesn't matter whether I took care of you guys then or now. Either way it's one, two, three!" barked the man who had followed them through the park.

"And you guys wrote the ransom note?" asked Marcus.

"Yeah, but we didn't do it for the money. I mean the ransom money," the tall man explained.

"Huh?" Marcus responded sounding somewhat confused.

"We did it because that circus is our competition. Do you think we'll ever let the Black circus top our show? Not as long as we're in control of the money and power. We tried to control that clown act, the Black circus, by buying it out but they said no. It's just like those music video channels. We control them, so we control the clown acts that go on them," said the tall manager.

"But the ransom was one million dollars. That's a lot of money and you didn't want it?" Marcus asked sounding more confused than ever.

"That's chump change," said the circus store manager. "See this building, how much do you think it's worth?"

Marcus stood their baffled. "I don't..." he stuttered.

"And how about that one there?" the tall manager pointed to the building containing the circus store. "And how about the one over there?" the man pointed to another rooftop two blocks over. "And see that construction site," the man directed their attention to an empty lot where the frame of a building had already been erected. "We're putting up another building over there. Buildings like this go for hundreds of millions of dollars each. In fact, while we've been able to use the building for more than a year, we were just putting on the finishing touches of this building up until about a month ago. Every time we came in we had to wear hard hats. We've already occupied twenty-percent of the offices and relocated the main branch of our circus business and one of our record studios. You're looking at a massive multibillion dollar industry. It's about control of the resources. You control the resources and you control the power, and everyone else acts like a fool. See that crane," the man pointed to a moving crane working on the building under construction, "we're building civilizations while you fools worry about chains, diamond earrings and rims for your cars."

Havier felt that it was time for him to weigh in. "My ancestors built civilizations. They built the Great Pyramid in Egypt's Nile valley. They built the Great Wall of Nigeria which contained more stone than the Great Pyramid or more than ten Empire State buildings combined. The Great Wall of Nigeria is only second in size to the Great Wall of China. We were mining iron in southern Africa 40,000 years ago. We invented writing and the art of medicine. Imhotep was the true father of Medicine to whom Hypocrites paid tribute. Every doctor today takes the Hippocratic oath when they should really be paying tribute to Imhotep. We Black people did surgery on the eye and removed cataracts one thousand years ago. And even in the modern era we controlled global movements and economic establishments like that of Marcus Garvey's Universal Negro Improvement Association and his Black Star Line—a shipping company. Do you know that there's a hip-hop group named after Marcus Garvey's Black Star line? And KRS-One has already declared hip-hop as a nation at the United Nations and is planning to build a hip-hop city as we speak."

"Yeah, I know. We tried to get KRS-One under contract so we could control him, but he refused."

"That's because he's a free hip-hop artist," replied Havier.

"You are a smart young man. It's too bad, or should I say too good that these music video clowns don't know what you know," said the tall circus store manager.

"But somebody obviously knows about their history in the circus. That's why the Black circus owners refused to sell it to you," Havier said defiantly.

"Enough! Get rid of them!" yelled the tall manager.

The other four men marched Havier, Marcus and Zauditu to the edge of the roof. Desperate, Marcus said, "You know how much we know, but do you know how much the police know?"

This stopped the four men for a minute and the clown said, "What?"

The short circus store manager trying to sound bold said, "We practically own the police."

All of a sudden a police siren blazed down the street and the car sounded as though it had stopped in front of the building.

"Hey, check that out," the tall circus store manager said to the clown while he took hold of Zauditu.

The clown went to the roof edge and peered over. "It's the cops. One of them is in the car and one of them is running toward the main lobby. He just unbuckled his gun and came in the main entrance. If he's headed up this way, he'll be here in a few minutes. The cop car isn't blocking the parking garage. We can take the freight elevator down and make our getaway. The only problem is the boys and the girl. What do we do about them?" the clown asked.

"Take them with us," said the tall manager to the clown. "You three, this way," he said waving his weapon at Havier, Marcus and Zauditu.

The three followed his instructions and the five men began to force their captives toward the stairwell.

"We should just get rid of them," said the clown.

The tall manager replied, "There's no time to get rid of them now. Look, I got a couple of these young thugs in the music studio downstairs. I'll have one of the interns take them on a tour in the direction of the cops. The cops will meet them and catch them red handed. We'll be long gone in another city with a good alibi by then."

The tall manager dialed a number on his cellular phone, "Yeah, call the studio and tell the manager there to send the two rap artists to the lobby of the building on a tour with the intern. Do it now, it's important!"

The men forced Havier, Marcus and Zauditu into the stairwell.

The freight elevator headed toward the ground floor and the Wright brothers waited in anticipation. The elevator opened near another stairwell that led to the parking garage. The Wright brothers were forced to walk into the garage.

"What are we going to do with them?" asked the clown.

"Put them in the trunk," said the tall manager.

The Duplicitous Five were laughing and strolling toward their car. The tall circus store manager had the keys in his hand and had just pressed the alarm button. The man's black SUV flashed in the relatively dimly lit garage. Marcus felt that it was time to make a move. He turned around and lunged toward the man holding the key. By the time the man realized that Marcus was upon him, it was too late. Marcus reached for the keys and ended up swatting them from the man's hand. The keys hit the ground, made a clanging noise and slid across the garage floor.

"Hey, my keys!" the tall manager exclaimed as the keys slid under an unknown car.

"What are we going to do, I don't see the keys?" asked the well built man that had chased them through Central Park as he and the short circus store manager looked under cars for the keys.

"We'll just walk out of the garage and catch a cab up the block. When we're on the other side of town. I'll have one of our limo drivers come and meet us from the Harlem parking garage," said the tall man.

Havier and especially Marcus were surprised that these two meagerly dressed men owned so many businesses; including a parking garage in Harlem's Black community.

"And what are we going to do with them now?" asked the clown.

The tall manager said, "We can't bring them with us so we have to leave them here."

"Leave them here?" the short manager replied.

"Yes! They'll never believe two boys! You two," the tall store manager said to the Wright brothers as he pointed to the door that they had come through, "Go back inside the building and don't come out until we come back to get you. Lock the door when they go back inside."

Havier and Marcus complied as the men walked toward them. They entered the door and heard the "click" from the lock on the door. With the Wright brothers too far away to hear the Duplicitous Five, the short manager said, "But what about the girl?"

"Take her this way!" the tall manager shouted. He told the parking attendant to go home, and gave him a hefty tip. When he was gone, they forced Zauditu into a closet in the Parking attendant's office. The office was about twenty feet long by ten feet wide with several Plexiglas windows and the closet was barely large enough for Zauditu to fit into. After forcing her in, the tall manager pulled down the shades on all of the windows of the office and locked her in.

Meanwhile the Wrights had quickly decided what to do.

"Let's go out the front!" Marcus exclaimed while running toward the exit.

The Wright brothers bolted down the hallway. They ran through the main lobby, toward the front door and exited the building. They spotted the men walking quickly up the block. Just then another cop car pulled up to the entrance of the building and both of the officers got out and walked toward the main entrance.

"Sir! Sir! We're the Wright brothers. The acrobat Zauditu's kidnappers, the Duplicitous Five are getting away that way," said Marcus.

The other cop also heard Marcus and had gotten out of the car. The three officers pursued the suspects with the Wright brothers. The three cops ran after the Duplicitous Five and Havier and Marcus also ran after them. The cops gained on the clown, the man who had chased the Wright brothers in Central Park and the clown's manager and tackled them. But the two circus store managers were getting away. Havier and Marcus dashed after them. Havier was in hot pursuit of the tall manager and Marcus the short manager. Then with one big swoop, Havier and Marcus simultaneously tackled the store managers. The managers struggled to get away and the Wright brothers struggled for supremacy. The wrestling match went on for a few minutes. Finally, five police cars flew down the block and several officers jumped out.

"Get those men there," a familiar voice said. It was Captain James.

The officers grabbed the two managers. Several of the other officers helped to take control of the other men being restrained by the first officers on the scene.

"Thanks guys, we'll take it from here," Captain James told the three Black officers who had been the first to respond to the scene.

All of the other cop cars that had pulled up with Captain James had African-American and Latino officers in them. It was a sight to see. All of these brave men of African descent capturing the gang of kidnappers.

After about ten minutes, the officer who had gone into the building returned. He was a Caucasian officer and had restrained three Black men in riot handcuffs. One of the African-American men was dressed in black pants, a nice blue button down shirt and had a tie on. The other two had baggy pants hanging off of their waists, fake platinum chains, fake diamond watches and fake diamond earrings. They were wearing t-shirts that read, "Thugged out Bucks."

"I found these three in the building. They said they were rappers about to get a contract from some company, and that the one in the blue shirt was taking them on a tour. And guess what the tour was of, the lobby. They've got to be lying because no one goes on or takes someone on a tour of a lobby. I bet they're involved in…"

"Un-handcuff them now!" Captain James commanded.

"But they might be involved in the…" the officer wasn't able to finish his sentence.

"Let them go. That's an order!" Captain James asserted and the subordinate officer un-handcuffed the young Black men.

"One of the Duplicitous Five set him up. That guy," Marcus pointed at the tall circus store manager. "He made a call to someone in his record studio. He told them to have an intern at the record company take two of its artists on a tour of the building and lobby so that they would be blamed for Zauditu's kidnapping," Marcus explained.

"And it almost worked. What a shame, our young brothers being set up like this every day," said Captain James.

"Yeah," Havier agreed.

"Where's Zauditu?" asked Captain James.

"I'm not sure. I think she's somewhere in the building."

"Go and get her out," Captain James told two of his officers.

"I got a call from your father right after he got out of a press conference. I was in a meeting in lower Manhattan. So, I left the meeting early and I sent two squad cars that were patrolling the area right away. Then I headed up here as fast as I could with this five car police detail that was with me."

"They almost got away," said Havier.

"But the important thing is we got them. I would like to personally thank you Havier and Marcus for saving Zauditu's life and the Black circus. We couldn't have solved the case without you. By the way, how did you find out the crooks were here?"

Havier and Marcus told Captain James about the school fair and rooftop pictures. They told him about the green circus shoes and that they could be found in Suite 102-B of the eleventh floor of the building. They also told him all of the other details that helped them to solve the crime. After hearing this, Captain James sent two officers up to block off the suite of offices until detectives could arrive to secure the evidence.

"It's pretty amazing how you solved the case. Look, I want to compile all of the evidence against the Duplicitous Five before we release it to the media. Then I'm going to call a press conference and I'm going to invite you two, so be ready," Captain James said as he was leaving.

Zauditu who was now safe in one of the officer's police cars, got out and thanked the Wright brothers before leaving with Captain James.

"I am so thankful that you two found me," she said.

"No problem," Havier said humbly.

"No really, it was a wonderful thing that you two just did."

"Thanks Zauditu, but we're just glad that you're safe," said Marcus.

"Maybe you guys will get a reward."

"Knowing that you're safe is reward enough," Havier replied.

"Take care, guys," Zauditu said with a smile as she got into the police cruiser.

"Take care, Zauditu!" the Wright brothers said in tandem.

"See you later, Captain James," Havier and Marcus said while waving to the police detail.

After all of the officers had left, the two rappers were still standing there, baffled and afraid to go back into the record studio.

"Peace," Havier greeted them with an African handshake.

"What was up with that?" one of them asked Havier.

"It's a big case that just went down. They thought you were involved. It had to do with this clown that kidnapped an acrobat from the Black circus," Marcus said impulsively.

"Word! That case has been all over the news," said the rapper.

"Yeah, and they thought they could take you down for it!" Marcus exclaimed.

"For real?" said the rappers together.

"Word is bond!" Havier replied.

"What's the meaning of that shirt?" Marcus asked the rappers.

"Well, you know," the rapper didn't have a logical explanation.

"Because anytime you call yourself a buck you are calling yourself what they called us on the slave plantation. They called us bucks and we were treated like animals. And we're not thugs either. Brother, we built great civilizations in Africa and now we're not building anything," said Marcus.

Havier was astounded at his brother's response. He had never heard Marcus speak this way. He waited for a minute and then added to what his brother had just said, "That's right, we built civilizations such as Mali that had virtually no crime on the streets. Ibn Battuta traveled to Mali and said that it was safe and that Black people there hated thievery and injustice. Ibn Battuta told a story of a valuable item that someone had found on the street and the King of Mali told the person who found it and turned it in to put it right back where he found it. The King wasn't worried about it being stolen. Can you imagine someone finding a wallet or purse on the streets today and putting it right back in the place it was found? It would be gone in a second! But in Mali, we had that much respect for law, order and humanity. Do you know that those cats who we just took down own this building and the record studio you were just in?"

"And they own that one too plus many more buildings," Marcus interjected while pointing.

"They're controlling our art by promoting the most negative parts of hip-hop culture. Black music has always been our saving grace. Even on the slave plantation we were singing about being free," said Havier.

"For real?" one of the rappers said.

"Yeah and there was another point in our history where whites humiliated us. They dressed us in blackface and humiliated us in minstrel shows. Now they have sissified the Black man with all of these diamond earrings in these rap videos." After he said this Havier glanced over and realized that Marcus was not wearing his fake diamond earring and Havier was glad to see this. "See they got us focused on the shine—earrings, chains and rims—while they own all the property, the businesses, many of the record companies and almost all of the avenues of distribution. It's a shame how they're controlling us. Hip-hop is much more than just about rapping and money, it is a whole culture that includes Emceeing, DJing, B-Boys and B-Girls, graffiti art, street knowledge, street language, street fashion, beat boxing and street entrepreneurialism," said Havier.

"I'm feeling you, but I write the kind of rhymes that I want," the rapper responded.

"Do you write what you want, or what is popular? Do you write about African history that will uplift Black and Latino people or about unattainable wealth? Most of the groups in the 1980's and early 1990's rhymed about being free, and embraced all aspects of hip-hop culture. Many of them rhymed about Black history and Black empowerment. That's almost gone from rap," said Havier.

"I'm feeling that, but where should I start?" the rapper said.

"Buy a copy of the *Autobiography of Malcolm X* and read it. Then go to a Black book vendor on the streets, or go to the Black history section of the bookstore or library and read as many books as you can. On the slave plantation they didn't want us to read and they still don't. Then listen to the hip-hop artists of the 1980's and early 1990's and even the artists of the 1970's and you will get a better understanding brother," Havier said warmly.

With that the Wright brothers gave the two young rappers an African handshake and headed home. They were thankful that they had finally saved Zauditu and solved the case.

Chapter 25: True Fame

Mr. and Mrs. Wright congratulated Havier and Marcus when they returned home and told their parents the news. Mrs. Wright said that she was so proud of her sons. Mr. Wright said that he would be sure to go to the press conference so that he could photograph it.

After school on Monday afternoon, the phone rang and Marcus answered it.

"Hello, this is Captain James, may I please speak to Havier or Marcus," he said.

"Yes, this is Marcus."

"We're going to have a press conference tomorrow afternoon at 4:30pm. It will be in front of the precinct. All of the prominent Black and Latino politicians and leaders will be there."

"We'll be there!" Marcus excitedly replied.

"See you guys there!"

"Havier, guess what? The press conference is tomorrow afternoon. That was Captain James and he wants us at the precinct at 4:30pm tomorrow."

"Word?"

"Yeah, and all of the Black leaders and politicians will be there," said Marcus.

"We should call Dad. He wants to photograph it."

"Ok, I'll call him," Marcus said as he picked up the phone. "Hi Dad, the press conference is tomorrow. You knew about it? Ok, see you when you get home."

The remainder of that Monday and Tuesday seemed as though it went by so slowly. Containing their excitement, the Wright brothers dressed in their nicest suits and ties for the press conference and headed over to the precinct after school.

When they arrived, many others had also gotten there including Mr. Wright, Zauditu, the district attorney and the media. They were greeted warmly by Captain James.

"Glad you guys could make it. I have good news, the clown's fingerprints were found on the other knife which really had Zauditu's blood on it. There were some minute clothing fibers on the knife from the costume she was wearing that night. Initially, the forensic cops had stored them, but didn't have any reason to assume that they were important. The other knife that Ralph had used with Zauditu's sister had different fibers with a different texture and color than the one used by the duplicitous five's clown. What that means is that we will be able to use the knife that he used against Zauditu as evidence.

"We also found the clown's fingerprints on the door of the boxes under the elephants, and on the clown shoes. The clothing and fingerprints of the man who chased you in the park and the clown's assistant were found on the chair used to bind Zauditu. Lastly, the two circus store manager's fingerprints were found on the ransom note," he said with a smile. The press conference will be starting shortly. I'm going to speak first, then Zauditu will speak, then the district attorney and then you two," said Captain James.

"Sounds good to me," Havier exclaimed.

In all, the press conference took about forty-five minutes. Havier and Marcus were sure to say Zauditu's name in most of the statements they made so that the public would no longer view her as just 'the acrobat'. After the conference they spoke to a few people for a short while. The Wright brothers were anxious to see the coverage of the press conference on the six o'clock news so they headed home.

They sat on the edge of their chairs when the news came on. The news anchor spoke, "Tonight the kidnappers of the acrobat from the Black circus have been apprehended. And the district attorney has obtained an indictment in the case. For this breaking story, we'll go to the police precinct where a press conference was just held."

The news broadcast switched to another reporter standing in front of the now empty police precinct steps. He began to speak, "A short while ago the district attorney and one of the police department Captains announced that those responsible for kidnapping the Ethiopian acrobat had been captured."

The news report switched to some of the video taken at the press conference. The image was that of the district attorney and Captain James standing next to each other.

The district attorney spoke first, "Today we secured an indictment against five of New York City's most dangerous criminals. These men were five of the city's businessmen and now they are going to be brought to justice."

"The men were apprehended this weekend as they tried to escape from their corporately owned buildings in the city. They were caught red handed. But the best part of this happy ending is how they were caught," Captain James emphasized.

The news reporter came back on, "That's right and you would never believe how the acrobat was found. Two young brothers, Havier and Marcus Wright helped the police department solve the case. In fact, in the Captain's words they are, 'Two of the greatest detectives that the city has ever had.' Here is what the Wright brothers said at the conference."

The news report switched to Marcus who was so ecstatic to see himself on television that he yelled out, "That's me!"

Havier replied, "See, I told you that you didn't have to be some clown in a music video to get on television."

Marcus and Havier listened to what the news report had included from what they had said at the press conference. Marcus was on the news first and said, "We located Zauditu, the acrobat and also captured the suspects by following a complex web of clues."

Havier spoke next in the news report, "We followed the trail from a set of images that we had photographed during Zauditu's disappearance. At one point in time, it looked as though we would never find Zauditu."

The field reporter came back on, "But they did find the acrobat." He glanced down at some notes he was holding in his hand, "Zauditu, yes the acrobat Zauditu was found by the two courageous young Wright brothers."

The next day almost all of New York's daily newspapers ran the story on their front pages. One of the newspaper headlines read, "Courageous Young Detectives Nab Acrobat Zauditu's Kidnappers." Strangely, all of the articles discussed Zauditu by using her name. The Wright brothers had influenced the media in New York City. A media that, until this time, was only able to see Zauditu as something less than a person by not mentioning her name.

"We're going to be known all over the city!" said Marcus.

"See, I told you young brother, I told you."

The papers also ran a story on how the Wright brothers had been harassed by Officer Thompson and Officer McNamara in the precinct. It featured the picture taken by Mr. Wright of the corrupt cops leaving the precinct the day they had harassed the Wrights.

That Friday the Wright brothers' report cards were sent home. Havier and Marcus both received grades of 'A' in all of their classes. Mr. and Mrs. Wright were both very happy that their sons had done well in school that marking period.

Now, with the case over, Havier and Marcus went to the circus during its final weekend in New York City. All of the acts were in their original form. Ralph the Magnificent Magician had rejoined the circus. His smoke puff act was incredible to watch again—even if the Wright brothers knew how it was done.

"Bang!" one acrobat disappeared and then reappeared with another "Bang!" It was amazing to watch the Black circus emerge from misery. The Wright brothers even saw Zauditu flipping and spinning in the air. The entire event was magnificent.

After the final performance, the two detectives went down to speak to the circus clowns, acrobats, other performers and management. All of them thanked the Wright brothers for finding Zauditu including Ralph and Jake. They thanked the circus members for entertaining them over the years and for tolerating them during their investigation.

The Wright brothers inquired about the third knife that contained Ralph's fingerprints, a bunch of nicks, but had no blood on it. Ralph explained that he had used the knife with nicks to practice throwing before the trick. The knife with Makeda's dried blood had been used in the knife throwing incident where she got cut. The last knife was never touched by him. That was the one used by the clown to stab Zauditu.

Havier and Marcus also asked Jake and Ralph why they ran from them. Both of them said that they had received telephone threats from some caller saying that if they shared anything with them that they would be killed. Jake, being a much more nervous person, got very anxious after hearing this and that's why he acted the way that he did. The caller assumed that no one else knew how Ralph did his tricks, except Jake. That's why he threatened Jake and Ralph so that they wouldn't give away any information that would lead to their capture.

Ralph said that the caller claimed that he was watching his every move, but that the caller sounded like a White man. Ralph also explained that he had seen the clown's foot and part of his clothing during the show. After seeing the clown, he sent them to the circus store with the riddle. He put the clue in a riddle because he thought that the circus might have been infiltrated by a spy and/or through some sort of technological device like a bug. The clue was one that only a Black man from Harlem would be able to decode.

Ralph explained that as the Wright brothers continued to follow them, the threats increased. The day that he was going to the park he was planning to put on a performance for some of the park patrons. Ralph explained that he did this from time to time to earn a little extra money. However, he received a call on his cellular phone about four hours before he headed to the park.

On his way to the park, Ralph was chased by a well built White man who turned out to be the same man from the Duplicitous Five that had followed and chased the Wright brothers from the circus store. Ralph got away using his smoke cloud magic trick, ran through the park and settled at the normal place that the circus entertainers congregated. Once he was at that location in the park, Ralph felt much more at ease but decided to take further cover in the woods. Finally, he felt relaxed and began to think out loud until he saw the Wright brothers. Because they showed up in the park right after the man had chased him, Ralph began to think that the two detectives were somehow working with the person who called him and the one that had just chased him. That's why he ran from them in Central Park. He explained that he made his escape not by running across the field, but by doubling back in the direction from which he had originally come. The clouds of smoke that he had created concealed him enough so that he could appear to be running across the field, and then he doubled back through the woods, ran past the pond, and exited through the park entrance.

The Wright brothers asked Ralph what he meant when he said that he couldn't believe that he 'did it' for the money. Ralph explained that he had gotten greedy for a special magic trick right after Zauditu's disappearance. As a result of this greediness, he inappropriately pressured Mary for a share of Zauditu's life insurance money and pressured Eric to encourage Mary to give him some money.

Ralph explained that the Duplicitous Five got their information from Jake and Eric who often bought things from their circus store. Being the talkative person that he is, Eric had shared an overt amount of information about the circus with the two circus store managers. The last time the circus was in town, he had told them about the life insurance policies of most of its members, including Zauditu's $1,000,000 policy. He also shared much about the layout of the circus and mistakenly told them about Ralph's magic act and Jake's role with the elephants.

They also spoke to Eric and Mary that day. They wondered what venture they were talking about while concealed in Eric's tent. Eric explained that they were talking about the four circus employees who had always stuck together during the difficult times and now all wanted their share of the money. When Havier noted that they had mentioned five people who had expected to get some of the insurance money, he received an acceptable clarification. Eric and Mary explained that the three others were supposed to be Ralph, Jake and Zauditu's sister Makeda. All five of them, with the exception of Makeda who had gone home, were relatively close to one another. Marcus pointed out that the coincidence of five people being involved was similar to the Duplicitous Five and this was what made he and Havier suspect them even more.

Glad that they had all of these explanations, the Wright brothers went home. A later check of Ralph's and Jake's phone records by Captain James confirmed that the Duplicitous Five had threatened them.

When they arrived home, their mother and father congratulated them again for saving Zauditu and for their good grades. All of the praise made the Wright brothers feel good about what they had done. Havier and Marcus Wright had emerged as two of New York's revered heroes with excellent grades. They had realized their potential as young Black men in a world that was often hostile to the expression of the realities of the African-American and of the African diaspora. The Wright brothers had become expert detectives and with this they went to sleep.

A few days later, while sitting in their living room waiting to go to a poetry show they heard a "Bang!, Bang! Bang!"

"Did you hear that Hav? Let's go check it out!" Marcus said as he bolted to the door.

Havier wanted to stop his brother, but he could not. "Marcus that could be gun shots!" he said running after him.

"Could be? I think it was!"

"Hold up Marcus!" Havier pinned his brother against the wall in fear that he would get hurt.

"Hold up for what? I want to see what just happened."

"No, wait a few minutes Marcus. It could be dangerous out there. Those were real gun shots!" Havier said as he eased off of his brother somewhat, but barricaded himself between his brother and the door.

The Wrights stared at one another for several minutes. The silence was periodically broken by the Wrights' heavy breathing. Marcus was breathing heavily because he had tried to push past his brother and Havier because he had resisted.

Within about two minutes police and ambulance sirens screamed down the block. "Let's go now! It's safe!" Marcus protested.

"No, wait another minute or two." Havier said calmly behind a deep breath.

Finally, after about seven minutes had passed, Havier allowed his brother to reach for the door. As the Marcus opened the door and peered out he saw an ambulance driving off and a slue of police cars. They were several blocks away in an intersection. From the Wrights' brownstone, it was hard to determine exactly what had happened.

"Let's go check it out!" Marcus pushed.

"No Marcus. That could be a very dangerous situation. We need to let the police do their job like Mom, Dad and Captain James just told us to do. We can speak to the Captain later and see if he needs our help.

Fortunately, Marcus accepted this explanation and the Wrights retreated to their living room. Little did they know, but another case would soon fall into their laps. In fact, it was closer now than ever and if you would like to know what happened you would have to read The Wright Brothers, The Case of the Officer Shot Down.

Afterword

This volume was written to demonstrate the need for more underground hip-hop culture and less corporate rap music. The culture of hip-hop was created in Bronx, New York in the early 1970's as a way to gain victory over the streets. It involved more than just rapping and more than music. It was a way of life that allowed one to avoid becoming a thug or drug dealer. Unlike much of the corporate rap of today, hip-hop culture did not glorify these lifestyles in mass. In fact, for about a decade after the creation of hip-hop there were no music television videos to characterize it in a negative light. Instead, the art form was celebrated on the streets of New York's Black and Latino communities. Hip-hop meant victory over negative life styles, a positive way to affirm one's identity, celebration, unity and an understanding of Black history.

During the second half of the 1980's, the art forms of KRS-One and Public Enemy dominated not only the musical landscape but also the street language of hip-hop. These artists created a true dialogue about the realities of Black life. People of African descent in America's cities engaged one another in discussion about the topics raised by these artists. KRS-One's songs "You Must Learn" and "Why Is That?" encouraged people of African descent to study their history and to become proactors when learning in a Eurocentric educational and social environment. Similarly, Public Enemy's song "Don't Believe the Hype" became a household phrase in the Black community. This language stood as a social commentary on the political events of the day and even positively influenced independent film maker Spike Lee. Lee made Public Enemy's "Fight the Power" the theme song for his movie "Do The Right Thing." If the reader would stop and reflect for a moment on the aforementioned titles and their meaning, he/she may find them in striking contrast to today's corporate rap music. Doing the right thing in the Black community meant fighting the power of oppression, learning African history and constantly questioning and reevaluating mainstream information that was taught in schools.

Hip-hop in the 1970's, the 1980's and first half of the 1990's was not devoid of self-serving capitalistic language. Instead, the glorification of antisocial behavior often stood on the fringe of the music and was greatly offset by conscious art. Even the language of hip-hop groups that bragged about having multiple partners and about smoking marijuana was underpinned by Black consciousness. This can be seen in the music of Tribe Called Quest, Bran Nubians, Das Efex, The Fugees and Pete Rock and C.L. Smooth.

During the late 1980's and early 1990's "gangster rap" emerged. This art form glorified the violent gang life that was too often a reality in Black and Latino neighborhoods. Yet, hip-hop remained a balanced art form throughout the early 1990's. The voices of KRS-One and Public Enemy still set the mark for discourse in the art form. However, as the 1990's elapsed, corporations became aware that Black consciousness in our music had to be stopped. Thus the corporate establishment promoted artists that helped to further popularize gangster rap and ushered in the money hungry, capitalistic, self-serving "bling-bling" era.

This new era of rap music stamped out other elements of hip-hop culture. For example, it eliminated or downplayed break dancing, DJing and live MC performances, as important aspects of the culture and highlighted the individualistic pursuit of wealth, gangster rap and the rap video. These artists utilized music videos to brag about how much money they had, yet often lacked the live street talent that defined hip-hop culture in the years preceding.

The bling-bling era was pushed by corporations and within a few years, the conscious music and culture that formerly dominated the genre was forced into small club venues and became known as "underground" hip-hop culture. Once the bling-bling era of hip-hop took hold during the late 1990's, it became the dominant mainstream expression of music. Thus the radical message of the 1980's and early 1990's was all but stamped out by corporations.

At the turn of the century, conscious music that focused upon love for the African community and anger toward the establishment was still being produced, but it was not promoted in mass by major corporations. Instead, these record companies began to dictate how many conscious uplifting songs could be on an album and the limit was often one. Even wealthy Black music moguls who had an influence on the industry chose to speak out of both sides of their mouth. On one hand, they encouraged positive hip-hop discussion forums, while they promoted the worst of the music and culture. Artists were duped into signing contracts that forced them to relinquish control of their albums to music executives and their corporations. Rappers were given contracts that offered comparatively small sums of money up front for the copyrights of their music and a promise to produce several albums for the music company. Music moguls, both Black and White, could then decide when to release an album of those that the rapper had agreed to produce. Too often an artist's album remained unreleased because of a corporate executive's decision to leave the album in limbo. At the same time the artist could not fulfill his/her contract that required him/her to release a series of albums because he/she has not yet released the first album. Thus, many artists' music is sitting on the dusty shelves of corporations to this day and the musicians cannot distribute any new music independently or through other companies because their contracts legally bind them from production and distribution of their own art. In fact, artists often must pay millions of dollars to corporations to release them from their contracts. However, without having any source of income, other than live performances, many of these artists are unable to generate enough income to satisfy these contracts.

A student of mine who worked for Black Entertainment Television (BET) described a music video scene. Jewelry, chains and diamond earrings are often brought in and placed on the artists during rap videos. The same over sexualized rap video dancers are brought in and are also exploited. Then, at the end of the video, the chains are removed and the rappers go home. This amounts to the sale of a lie because our youth often believe that the artists have permanent access to that wealth.

Some people have compared the current state of hip-hop to that of heavy metal music. Others compared gangster rappers like Biggie Smalls to actors like Arnold Schwarzenegger in Terminator 2. These comparisons are not fair for several reasons. First, and foremost the Black community lives much closer to the reality of violence which is discussed in corporate rap. Thus, when rappers promote violence in their music, they are establishing a norm for youth who honor them to follow. In this case, art reflects reality much more among Blacks than among Whites who listen to heavy metal.

Others have argued that Whites are the biggest consumers of gangster rap, with numbers in the White/Black consumer category being 80/20 percent respectively or even higher. With many albums this is true. I have seen Whites imitate the dancing and clothing styles of Blacks in these albums. But at the end of the day, the communities that they return to are overwhelmingly not plagued by violence. So even if Whites today purchase the majority of a given music album and imitate antisocial behavior in a club setting, they return to communities with an economic, political, social and educational power base. On the other hand, a large percentage of Blacks among the 20% who purchase a given bling-bling, gangster rap album return to communities that are riddled with violence and whose families and social institutions are not nearly as strong as those of European Americans. To further complicate matters, corporate sales of albums do not take into account the underground market sales of bootlegged music that exists primarily in the Black community. Something that would tip the scales of Black/White listeners from the 80/20 category to a more even balance of listenership.

Others argue that rap artists have a right to freedom of expression. However, African-American music has always been used as a method of expressing one's discontent and protesting against oppression. Even on the slave plantation enslaved Black people sang African spirituals which encouraged enslaved Blacks to escape and others to plan outright revolt against their masters.

Other African-American art forms such as Blues, Jazz, R&B and Rock and Roll all served the community as a way to promote cohesiveness and resistance against unfair social, economic and political conditions. Gangster rap and bling-bling rap do none of this. Instead, they glorify capitalism and its children individualism and white supremacy. It cares nothing for the community, an African centered belief system, and encourages one brother to dog another just to get ahead. This is exemplified in the perpetual statements by bling-bling era rappers who say, "Don't be mad because I have…" And anytime one questions their contradictory behavior they are accused of "hating."

But they have missed the mark. The community is not mad because these artists have or desire to live a nice lifestyle. Instead, the community is furious because these artists do not give people the tools to achieve the same lifestyle that they have. They do not tell people about the hard work that it took to become who they have become, and the reality of their true economic situation.

Fortunately, KRS-One and others have organized a movement for the spiritual upliftment of all hip-hop artists and fans. Through the Temple of Hip-hop KRS-One has reached millions of people worldwide. He continuously produces music which creatively instructs its listener on the different elements of hip-hop and how he/she can better his/her life. Whether you are a parent or a young man or a young woman reading this book, we must collectively realize that it is mandatory to teach our children and each other these lessons about hip-hop from the time that they can speak and understand. Otherwise, corporate rap will influence them negatively and even might control them. KRS-One is also an author and lectures at major universities. His shows are the most interactive shows that exist and one always leaves his presence with a deeper understanding of herself/himself and the world.

Although this volume describes a critical moment in time for the Black community, it is my hope and desire that it shall remain just that. I truly believe that we will look back upon this time period as one of serious error. However, I believe that we shall be looking back from the standpoint of victory over the streets and while being in harmony within the Universe as well as God's and the Ancestor's positive vision for us.